Chicano

Sheila O'Malley

Sheila O'Malley Publishing

ASPEN

CHICANO

Published by Sheila O'Malley

Aspen

ISBN:0692243860
ISBN-13:9780692243862

Library of Congress Control Number: 2014912800

Printed in the United States of America

Chi·ca·no

noun \chi-ˈkä-(ˌ)nō *also* shi-\ : an American and especially a man or boy
of Mexican descent

CONTENTS

ACKNOWLEDGMENTS

Many thanks are necessary, as the people in my family and in my life have made it possible for me to endeavor to write and to live in some amazing places. To my sons - Gabriel, Stefan and Shealen – you are my constant joy and I am proud of each of you. To my grandchildren - Kaitlyn, Daniel, and Caidenn – what a bright future our world has with all of you in it! To my dad and mom, Jon and Sharon Mulford, you have been there for us every step of the way. And especially to my mom, Sharon Mulford, who edited the text in its entirety. To Jeff Lambert, my dearest of friends, you too have been there helping us along on our path, sometimes paving it ahead of us. To Jael Herrera, who provided a sounding board for my Spanish quips and advice during brainstorming. To my brother, Phil Feller, and to Bettyjo Stallsworth, for all your advice and input. To my entire family – Laurel, Mark, Matt, Andrea, Phil and Nick – because we have been there for each other and always will be.

Mexican / Arizona Border

CHAPTER 1

COYOTES

The space is cramped. I have to keep my head turned sideways to see my mother. She is cuddling my baby sister, speaking soothing words to her. Although there is nothing frantic in her manner, I know she must be feeling desperate. The man with the scar had said he would kill Elena if she makes any sounds as we cross the border. My mother knows nothing but love will keep the child quiet during this grueling trip, with the floorboards above us keeping us pinned to the truck bed.

It is hot. My forehead is wet and dripping. My stomach is hungry. I do not say a word. My hand moves to my shirt pocket, where my mother's note to me is safe. I can barely make out the outline of its crumpled edges with my finger. It is something very important for me to read and learn later, once I have gotten away.

As we bounce along in the heat for countless hours, my mother speaks to me in hushed tones. She goes over the plan with me. *"Mijo, quédate aquí hasta que bajen los demás. Luego bajate despacito y escondes cerca las llantas. Cuando nadie esta mirando, ¡corre lo más rápido que puedas! No le hace que te oyes. ¡Sólo corres y no te fijas!"* My mother wants me to stay here in this space until all the other people get off. She wants me to hide by the tires and to run off when no one is looking. No matter what I hear, I am not to look around, just run. Her words make me feel afraid and sad, yet I trust her conviction. I know there is something wrong; I can feel it.

My head aches. The small pack my mother insisted I wear is beginning to poke into my wet backside. My mother continues to whisper words of advice to me as my sister sleeps. She tells me she has only packed underclothes for me, and I am to change them when I encounter water to wash the others. She tells me my *tia* Maria has packed her *pan blanco* for me. It is my favorite, a lightly sweet small white loaf of bread, and my Aunt Maria's is the best around. Mother tells me to only sip the water in my pack, but to drink heavily when I find water and to refill the little bottle in the pack. My head is swimming with instructions but I listen carefully.

She slips two corn husks into my hand and pats my fingers. *"Come sólo uno mijo y ahorras el otro."* I put one *tamal* into my pack, carefully keeping its wrap around it. The other I begin peeling back the husk to stuff its warm contents hungrily into my mouth. I know she is right, that I should save the other, but I am so hungry!

The jolting and rumbling of the truck suddenly stops. We are on a smoother road now and it is much more comfortable. A slight breeze can be felt as the truck seems to pick up speed. All of the rugs piled over us above the wood floorboards of the truck do not allow for much air to reach us down here in our crawl space. To look at the truck, you would never guess there were 30 people crammed together at its base. When they had opened the tailgate, all you could see were folds of rugs piled high. The men had us climb over the rugs to a spot in the center where a man held up small square of wood covered by a rug. Down here, he had pointed, urging us to move quickly by a quick smack to whatever body part his hand managed to swat. Once we were all in, a thud was heard above us and complete darkness enveloped the space.

I cannot see my father. He is shielded by my mother's body but I can make out his arm wrapped over my mother's stomach. He has been quiet the entire trip and I hope he is asleep. The land he has worked so hard to cultivate has been given away to the man with the scar in trade for this passage to America. Our *terreno* given away: it seems a lot to give but my father says we will have a good life and he smiles when he talks of life across the border. It is nice to see my father smile.

The truck has been stopping and then moving in short spurts for a long time now. Our space is even hotter now, and I feel sick with hunger and heat. I can smell the acrid exhaust from the truck and I long for it to move faster. I want to sleep but I am afraid to; I want to watch my family. I wait for my mother to speak to me. My sister begins to sniffle. My eyes widen in fear. My mother finds a *chupón* and places it in her mouth. Elena suckles it earnestly and I see her eyes roll back as she falls back to sleep.

My mother was our village *curandera*. She is a great healer. She has shown me the plants and herbs from which she grinds powders and makes poultice. She told me she has placed one of her *bolsas de medicina* in my pack, so I can cure myself if needed. As I begin to make a mental checklist of the contents of my pack, my eyes close. Her medicine bags will be useful. I begin a silent inventory of what I hope she has packed.

Loud talking and truck doors banging wake me. My mother's eyes are looking at me. The edges crinkle and I know she is smiling at me in the darkness. She touches her finger to her lips. She will not be giving me instructions or speaking to me. The truck lurches forward and I can hear the gears grind. We are moving faster and I can even feel a slight breeze.

We are in total darkness. I can't see forms but I can hear the gentle breathing of my mother and sister. Men begin to talk in muffled tones which seem far away. The truck is moving slowly and is bouncing along on rough ground. It is cool in the space. Suddenly, I feel my mother's hand grab mine. *"Mijo escúchame bien. La mochila - ¡nunca la deje fuera de su vista!"* She whispers this fiercely but only so I can hear. I hold the pack straps tightly. My mother has been teaching me things to keep me alive, so something about my pack is important if I am to never let it out of my sight.

The truck grinds to a halt and the voices get louder. *"¡Bájense! ¡rápido!"* the men scream as they pound the sides of the truck. I know what I have to do but I am afraid. There is now fresh air pouring down on me and I can see stars through the square opening above us. A flashlight beam moves around us, and I hide my face and try to move to the side when I see it, hoping it will not catch me.

People begin to exit through the opening. I cower to the side of the truck bed, making myself as small as I can. Soon I see the form of my mother moving toward the opening. I almost cry out but I bite my tongue. I know the plan and I know my mother is serious. I must do what she asks of me. I decide to shimmy toward the opening when I hear the voices move away from the truck. I don't want to be found by the flashlight beam and I don't want to be locked in this space. I move to the opening and slowly peer above its edge. No one is near the rugs and I can't see anyone at the tailgate. Slowly I lower myself over the tailgate and silently touch the ground. I roll under the truck and next to the back tire quickly. I can hear my breathing and I try to slow it. Too loud! I look around.

The men seem to be lining everyone up. I can see their legs from under the truck. A man is talking loudly but my heart is pounding in my ears and I cannot make out what he says. No one seems to be looking toward the truck so I creep away, slowly at first and then when I am sure no one will hear, I begin to run! I look over my shoulder because I am sure at any moment they will come after me. I hear gunshots and hear the sound of bundles thudding against the ground, as though thrown from the truck.

At first I wonder if they are unloading the rugs and then I know. The sound of my mother's voice enters my head: "*¡Corre ahora, llora después!* Not one to argue with my mother, I run even faster than before and this time I do not bother to look back. I could never go back. I will run now and cry later.

CHAPTER 2

NO GOODBYES

It is very dark and I know I cannot yet use the old compass my father taught me to read. My mother told me to head north and slightly west to get further into the United States and to go nearer to water. She told me of a river, *el rio de San Pedro*, will carry me northward and provide water. I am still running but it is not fast. The ground is rough and I stumble regularly. Fear keeps me going.

I begin to think of my pueblo. My father told me many in my country say that Naco is *"un pueblo chico, olvidado de Dios"* (A small village forgotten by God). When the man with the scar convinced my father to trade his land for passage to America, perhaps it was *un trato del diablo*. Since God has forgotten us, the devil can run amok making deals with poor farmers.

I seem to be walking in a gully, or a dry stream bed, since

the sides of the land are higher on both sides of me. I think on this. Perhaps the river to which I am headed uses this very land for overflow! Or maybe it once did. The lack of foliage all around me tells me there isn't much rainfall in this area. I don't know which way I am going and I pray I am not going south to Mexico. It will be hours before daylight, when the sun and my old compass will tell me the direction. I want to lie down and sleep but there is nowhere to hide and no way I want to be caught by the men in the truck!

This new thought sends adrenaline to my legs and I begin to run faster. What if the men in the truck discover I am missing? I know if I keep following this gully, it will lead me away from where I have been. Going in a circle is another danger I could face out here, so I decide right then to stay on this track. I look up at the stars. I can see *la osa mayor*. *"¡La cola de osa menor es norte!"* I say out loud. As I cover my mouth and look around frantically. I also smile to myself because now I can find north at night! Both large sets of stars above me are pointing to the star of the north! The tip of the little bear's tail is the north star!

Soon the gully diverges and one part seems to continue west, the other north. I choose to take the smaller one and try to go north. My legs are shaking. I don't know if it is fear, cold or exhaustion that is making them do it. I know I must stop soon but also know I need to get far away from those men. I see a mound where the sides of the gully are rising. I follow the track and climb up a steep embankment. There is a road here. I know this is not a good place for me to travel, even though it is flat. I turn to go back down into the gully and I see a flash in the distance. It looks like headlights coming! Now I am sliding, trying to quickly descend. I can feel my heart pounding in my chest. I dive behind the gully's small wall and try to lie flat. I am not far enough away from the road to get away from anyone if they see me, so they must not see me. I can hear a motor coming closer and whatever it is seems to be moving slowly. I see lights flash overhead and realize it is a flashlight sweeping over the land. I move as close to the dirt mound as I can, keeping as still and quiet as I am able.

As the sound moves nearby and then past where I am hidden, I make out the outline of the vehicle. It is a truck! I do not know for sure it is the men, but I feel it in my stomach and I am convinced it is. I remain on my stomach and move my way back down the gully, back the way I came at the fork. I will have to wait until later to turn north. "*Mi libertad es norte,*" I whisper to myself.

I feel safer now that I am walking away from the road. I am keeping the stars and my path aligned somewhat, so I can tell I am walking west by northwest. I know I am walking a longer distance because the gullies wind to and fro, but I can tell my course is steady and I feel I am making my mother proud.

Thinking of her makes me choke and stumble. I cannot afford to think right now. I can feel danger but I can barely see in front of me. I repeat "North to Freedom" in my head and continue to walk along carefully. *Mi libertad es norte.*

There are lights ahead. Dim ones, but I can see them in the distance. Instinctively I know I cannot go near those. Another gully turn-off is ahead and by the stars it heads due north. I know the road is there but perhaps I can cross the road? If I do this, I must keep low to the ground. I must be as a coyote, drawing no attention to myself. I feel the panic in my chest but I also feel a rush of energy I didn't know I could have. I head up this gully, steady and quiet. I keep watch in all directions as I near the slope upward. Once I am near the top of the hill and find the road, I get on my knees and scurry across the road, trying to mimic a small animal. On the other side I lie flat and roll down the embankment as fast as I can. I feel dizzy once I stop but I try to stay focused. I need to find somewhere to hide just in case!

I look up at the stars, get my bearings north, and run that direction as fast and quietly as I can. When I find a bush after running for what seems like forever, I stop. I listen. I cannot hear anything but the wind rustling gently across the ground. I find another gully in which to travel, and I feel grateful. *"Gracias Señor por sus bendiciones,"* I pray silently. I have heard my mother pray it a thousand times and I can hear her voice say it again. Thank you Lord for your blessings. Tears are choking me. I don't want to make noise! I must be a man. My father does not allow me to cry!

The Arizona Desert

CHAPTER 3

NORTH TO FREEDOM

My thoughts are now spinning me. I can barely think or see through my tears. I need to find somewhere to hide and sleep. If I sleep, I can try to shut out the noise in my head. I raise my head as I stumble over some rocks. There ahead of me is another steep embankment. It has to be a road. But it is a different road because the embankment is far steeper and the ground is now rock, small rock. As much as my grief has overwhelmed me and my fear has gripped my heart, I am resolved to climb and cross this road. I steel my mind, I force myself to concentrate on becoming as a small animal who crosses this road unnoticed and quickly.

My eyes are now wide as my surprise hits me. This is a large road, with paint markings which glow in the moonlight! I don't see any lights, so I run across it as fast as I can, careful to hunch over and use small steps. This time I opt to slide down the other side rather than roll. It is much steeper and I feel more in control going down this way. I see some trees ahead so I run for them. As I stand in solitude, hidden against a tree trunk, I close my eyes to think.

I can hear my mother's voice telling me to go northwest to the river. Mainly I have been going north so I realize I need to go west or northwest soon, so I can find this river. Once the sun rises, I will know where due west is but my travel will be more difficult. I don't want to risk being seen. My mother warned me a child alone will attract attention and she told me to never go with strangers. She told me to run from them and not allow them to capture me.

I slide down the trunk of the tree without realizing it. When I finally open my eyes, the sun is shining. My mouth feels very dry. I reach into my pack and pull out my bottle of water. I sip it carefully but I really want to drink it all. I know this is not wise until I can find water. My mother told me many stories and gave me many examples of how to capture water, but she told me it is not easy. Far better would be to focus and reach the river, and have a steady water source.

I slowly stand up and look around. I see the sun is still east, so I didn't sleep a long time. I resolve to travel northwest to accomplish both goals, water and freedom. I have to choose how to walk in the open unnoticed so I try to see if there are trees or gullies. I opt to follow a line of trees to my left and see how far it goes. It mainly is going north but it does seem to go slightly to the west. When I reach the last tree, I peek out to see where I can go to next. I see a large round gray building. I can't go toward it. I see off in the distance there is another line of trees, and they seem to head in a straight line. They are heading northwest! I take this as a sign, make a sign of the cross as a quick thank-you to God, and run toward them with all my might.

I am panting hard when I reach the first tree, so I stop to gather my wits and look around me. I don't see anyone else but I do see a road and that is what this line of trees follows. Although it concerns me somewhat, I remember it is a sign and a blessing from God. I take another sip from my bottle and start walking from tree to tree. There are so many places where the distance to the next tree seems a long way off, and I begin to worry about the trees disappearing altogether. Fortunately, I have not heard a single motor and have not seen a single person so far.

As if to calm my fears, the trees begin to appear closer together as I continue walking. I make a pattern of walking leisurely through the trees, and sprinting across open areas. All at once, while sprinting, I hear the sound of a motor. Someone is approaching! I am in the open and if I continue to run, I will surely be seen! I drop where I am and lay myself out flat. I am grateful to see a bush near me. I crawl ever so slowly toward its base and then am still. The sound grows closer and then further away as the vehicle speeds off into the distance. I feel sure I have not been found out. I get up cautiously and then run with all my might to the next grove of trees.

I hear another motor! Hidden behind a tree I don't feel as naked as I had in the field. This time I can see a blue car up on a different road, not the road near me by the trees. This newly discovered road runs next to my road! Once the car passes, I venture out to see what is there. I climb a short embankment to the smaller road. Further up a higher embankment is the other road. My curiosity will not let me stop until I have climbed up its embankment and am standing on its asphalt. It has the painted markings of the previous large road I had seen. From here I can also see taller and greener trees in the distance, directly west from where I stand.

The sun is now overhead but I had held my bearings because of my northwest line of trees. I have a decision to make and I must make it quickly. With that, I set off down the other side of the steep embankment and run toward the more lush trees. As I run, I suddenly hear another motor but this time it is over my head! As I look up, I have to stop. An airplane is flying over me! I hope they are not searching for a small boy who has escaped bad men. I begin to run faster than I had before, knowing I have to reach those trees to feel safe.

There are Cottonwood trees everywhere! *¡El jardín del Edén!* I have found the Garden of Eden! I creep carefully through the trees, still heading west. I need to find this river because my water supply is low. I know I am close because the lushness in which I travel is far greater than all of the miles I have walked before. My mind is giddy with the thoughts of food and water in abundance.

The thought of food has made me weak. I remember the *tamal* in my pack and sit next to a large cottonwood tree to rummage. I peel back the fresh corn husk. As I put each small morsel I pluck from the husk into my mouth, I think nothing has ever tasted so good. My mother's tamales are the best in our village, and I assume, the whole world.

Refreshed, I start again toward the west, to where the river should appear. The air is fresh, and I hear birds all around. I feel a peace I have not felt since I was last in my bed in *Naco*. This is a different peace. I feel a peace which is surrounded by surprise, wonder and the unknown. I am on an adventure and I feel it to my core.

I pull out my bottle and sip the last of its contents. I don't feel despair, but hope. I will fill it soon, I just know I will. My mother taught me to boil water, to kill disease and bacteria. She also told me not to build fires at night, for those fires can be seen from afar. It is nearing dusk and I feel a panic, so I run. I trip over a sturdy branch. I almost keep going but something makes me turn and look back at it. Such a sturdy branch would make a good walking stick. I bend over and pull it up. I begin to strip its smaller branches. Later I will smooth its wood, I think as I carry it with me.

There before me, glimmering in the setting sun, is a river of water. Tears invade my eyes as I run toward it. I try to have caution, the caution my mother taught me for water, but I find myself plunging into the water with abandon. It is cool and refreshing and I feel myself float. Carefully, I touch the ground beneath me and when I realize it is close, I allow myself to drift in the current. My walking stick is buoyant so together we ride this current as it lazily flows northward.

'*Mamá,* my washing is done,' I tell my mother in my mind. I smile as I float. Suddenly it occurs to me what might get wet in my pack. *¡Mis yerbas!* In my panic, I scramble to the nearest bank and crawl out under a tree. My pack is soaked and I am sick with the thought of losing all of my healing herbs and poultices. I pull out my bag of medicines. It is tightly bound. Inside, snug and dry, are tiny packets of herbs and powders. They were all safely bundled. *Mi mamá* had thought of everything. Inside the pack, I find all of my belongings were bound and wrapped carefully. I could float all day if I wanted! With great relief, I repack everything carefully. I fill my water bottle, even though I still have to find the means to boil it. *Dios proveerá,* I think to myself as I walk back into the river. I am learning. Yes, God will provide.

As the darkness descends, I wearily pull myself back out of the water. I must find a place to camp before I can no longer see. I can see a flat grassy area ahead with trees all around it and determine this is my spot. Thankfully it is warm and I am not yet regretting my wet clothing. I shed my outer clothing and choose to sleep in my underclothes. I carefully place my shirt and pants on tufts of grass so they can dry. I have not surmised if I will try to float or walk the next day, but this way I will have a comfortable choice.

The water in my bottle appears cleaner than the water at home, so I elect to drink it and refill the bottle before I settle to sleep. Tomorrow I will look for food. There are tufts of grass that surround me where I sleep, so I drift off knowing I will be unseen by my most dangerous of predators, humans.

CHAPTER 4

WHITE RABBIT

A pink object is making my eyes cross as I awaken. Looking at me intently is a white rabbit. *¡Conejo blanco!* I can't believe it. God's blessing again, the luck of a white rabbit! He hops away as I sit and rub my eyes. I am so hungry! I look into my pack. The *pan blanco*! My aunt's sweet white bread makes my mouth water as I unwrap its packet carefully. I pull it apart, trying to make a half. I will save the other half for later. Wrapping the saved part carefully, I survey the river area. Today I will walk and observe. I will need to find food. The river likely attracts an abundance of animals.

I love this walk! The beauty overwhelms me. The sounds intoxicate me. I have never been to such a place! It is like a dream. I am hungry though, so it is a dream from which I awaken rapidly. I survey the ground as I walk. I am hoping to find familiar plants my mother has taught me to gather.
I feel a branch flick my eye. How did I miss that coming! I hold it tight and pull it to my side. There dangling from the

branch is a mesquite bean! This is exciting! I can make flour or eat the bean! I begin to pluck the pods as fast as I can! I have found food and found it in abundance. I can barely contain my excitement. Once my pack is filled, I kneel in the muddy soil and bow my head to pray. Once again, my blessings have filled my heart beyond measure.

I keep walking along the banks, wondering if I should hop into the river. Ahead of me I hear a loud "snap!" I duck low into the grasses. I am gripped with fear but also trembling with excitement. What has just happened? I creep along, unable to stop my curiosity. I am quiet and careful, but I do want to understand whatever peril is ahead. I think I will creep up on it and then retreat once I understand the danger.

I am totally unprepared for what I encounter. There in my path is *el conejo blanco*, its foot impaled and trapped within metal teeth. I grab my pack and immediately search for the herb which makes feeling cease. I lightly touch the white rabbit's forehead and ears and make cooing sounds to ease its fear. I remember my mother doing this when my father broke his leg. I sprinkle the powder over the leg. I examine the metal trap, trying to figure out its release. Carefully I pull its teeth apart hoping the rabbit will be able to remove his leg. It does not move. I wedge my walking stick into the trap's teeth, and use one hand to gently lift the leg from its grasp. I lower the metal slowly and remove my stick at the same time. It makes a slight snap as I let go near the ground.

I carry the rabbit to a grove of trees. I gather willow and cottonwood sticks and quickly sort through them. I will need some pliable, but a few of them will need to be sturdy to act as a splint. I make two of the heartiest wood pieces into the splint, placed on either side of the broken leg. I use the pliable long pieces as a rope to twine the splint together.

Once I have a crude bandage in place, I open my water bottle and rinse the wound. Since it is not sterile, I add a poultice, which I quickly make from two herbs which have antibacterial properties and apply it thickly to the wound on all sides. I will need to make a fire soon. I need to make a tea, and having better water for drinking and cleansing wounds will be better for both of us. I choose to risk a fire but will find a spot in a thicker portion of the woods.

I carry my new friend to what I have determined to be our best option for a campsite, and make a bed of leaves for him. I then set out to gather small twigs. I place those in a fire ring I fashioned out of a hole and a few stones from the river's edge. Then I search for larger and drier pieces of wood. These I have to scour further to find but find them I do! Once I have the fire mound ready I find the packet my mother had wrapped. A few precious matchsticks are there, with a special tinder she used to make magic fire.

The fire glows and is cheerful. I pull out the small metal pot which served as the base of my pack. I run to the water and fill it. Carefully I place it on the fire's edge, where there are glowing embers. Once the water boils, I add the *yerba mansa* to make a pain-killing tea. I try to think of how to give this tea to a rabbit. I look through my pack. *¡Un chupón!* I cut the suckling part from the plastic base of the pacifier. I squeeze the bulb into the tea and pull it out - full of the pain reliever. I squirt this into the rabbit's mouth. I do this several times. Then I take the last of the tea, now cooled, and pour it over the bound wound.

I go and fill the metal pot once again. This time I boil it and carefully pour it into my bottle. I do this twice and then I boil water one more time and set it aside to cool. I begin to cover the fire on the sides to hide it from sight. I drink from the now cool pot and put it back into my pack. Then I curl up near the rabbit and the fire and fall asleep.

The rabbit is gone. I am beside myself with sadness. I want to give him a bean to eat. I want to check his dressings and help his wounds heal. I clean up the area and make sure my fire is out. I will continue on my path, following the river. I munch on a bean. My hunger is great and it is just what I need. Again, I reflect on the bean and how I want to give some to the rabbit.

The white rabbit is fortune. He came to me to bring me *buena suerte*. Good luck for *mi viaje* and my trip needs it. I pray he will heal quickly and that he will find many beans on his road to recovery. In my hunger, it never occurred to me to eat the rabbit. I have eaten many rabbits but my white rabbit is sacred to me. I wonder if I will ever eat another rabbit again.

Riparian Regions - San Pedro

CHAPTER 5

THE RIVER

The river looks inviting but my hope of encountering *el conejo* outweighs my desire to float along the river. If I can help my white rabbit, I will. My head is still thinking of food as I walk along the riverbanks, so I begin to search for stones to grind my beans. Images of *tortillas* dance in my mind. I imagine finding chili peppers and vegetables to stuff in them but I haven't seen anything on my path like those. A flat white stone catches my eye as I look into the stream. I wade out to see it. It is perfect. With this stone and one to grind against it, I can make my own mortar and pestle.. It won't be as artistic as my mother's *molcajete* but it will serve me well.

molcajete

Another stone, nearer to my shoreline, catches my eye. It is also white. My *molcajete* will match in color. As I retrieve the stone, I begin to look for a work area. It will need to serve as a campsite, since grinding will be a long process, and I will need to heat the tortillas, once I have made the *masa*. I will use some of the wild sunflower (its seeds) I found for oil. I also will need something in which to place my ground beans. I continue to walk the river. A large curved stone awaits me. It is as though providence placed it there.

I see a grouping of trees ahead with grasses in between, so I head there to see about accommodations. The area seems perfect, the trees large enough to shield my fire, and the area lush enough for my bed to be soft. I set down my pack and lay out my stones. I begin to grind the beans with my small grinding stone against my flat white stone. As I get a fine powder, I empty it into the large rounded stone. I repeat this for as long as my arms endure. When I can do no more, I sit and pull the seeds from my sunflowers.

To protect the flour and the seeds, I will need something to contain them. In my pack I have my tin of special mints. I put the mints in a plastic package with my underwear. This tin I use for the seeds. I can collect these seeds whenever I encounter the wild sunflowers. The flour will be more difficult. I have some brown paper from my Aunt's bread, but it is not large enough. I walk the area and try to imagine something I can use. Then I see it, the bird nest. It is tilted sideways and seems to be abandoned. I gently pull it from the branches. With the paper spread out it will hold my ground bean nicely. Once I fill it with the ground bean, I cover it with some leaves and carefully place it up against a tree, next to my pack.

I am too tired to build a fire this night, so I pull out a few beans to eat and then lie down in the grasses. The tortillas will have to wait until tomorrow. I leave out a bean for my white rabbit, although I have not seen him all day. I have hope.

Something wakes me. The night is very dark. Perhaps there is cloud cover. There it is, the sound that woke me. A crackling sound in the underbrush not far from me. Carefully I reach to pull the grasses near me over my pack and my day's labors. Thankfully I do not have much to cover and no fire to hide. I crouch behind the tallest grasses near the tree but I stay close enough to grab my pack if I have to run. I am wishing I had placed my ground beans inside my pack. Silently I wait and watch.

Suddenly my eyes can see its eyes staring straight at me. *"El ocelote"*, I whisper to myself. I know I have been spotted and my scent is impossible to cover. The ocelot is very small. I do not know much about it but I also know I cannot move. I don't feel fear. I had feared it was a man, so my relief invades my body. Soon it becomes bored of me and turns to the river. I feel a wave of sleepiness come over me I cannot fight. I gently drop down into the grasses next to my pack and fall fast asleep.

The morning sunshine warms me and I awaken to a cacophony of bird song. This makes me very happy. Remembering my wish from the previous night, I gently wrap and pack my previous days' labors into my pack. I resolve to carry the stones as well. I cannot be assured I will find them downstream and I really want the tools. Now more heavily burdened, I think seriously about floating in the river.

I wade into the river. It seems shallow to me. I hope it will carry me and my new weight with the ease I had traveled earlier. As I lie down in the river and allow my body to relax, I realize I am not moving. I stand and am now carrying a heavier cargo than before. I move back to the shore and start walking. As the day grows warmer, I feel better. I am beginning to dry, so I am lighter and my steps grow quicker.

The water seems deeper now, as I monitor it to my left. I can see the sun is still not overhead, so maybe I can still make some time floating and then dry off once again. I decide to try again. As I begin to float the current moves me this time. I close my eyes and feel the sun's warmth through the trees. My feet are aimed downstream. In case I encounter anything in the stream, my feet will touch it first. ·

When my eyes open next, the sun is shining brightly overhead. I glance around to get my bearings. The river is much wider now and I see a woman pointing at me from the bank! She looks horrified, so to ease her appearance, I smile and wave. Instantly she smiles and calls out. She is waving! I know I cannot stop and make this encounter so I close my eyes and hope I can drift past her quickly. Tonight I will sleep on the opposite shore.

I wait for as long as I can stand and then open my eyes again. I have gone under the canopy of trees again, and the sun is not as warm under it. My body makes a vague shiver, so I climb out of the stream. I had wanted to walk along the same shore as before, in case my white rabbit should appear. But for this day, I will remain on the other side.

I walk along the winding shoreline, and try to think about my chance meeting. I know if the woman reports seeing a young child floating in the river, it could be dangerous for me here. However, floating far away from her, she might not know how young I am. Perhaps she had since relaxed because I showed her I was all right and unafraid of my circumstance. I determine to travel by and near water is more important than worrying about the woman, so I keep traveling adjacent to the river. I do try to keep back into the trees somewhat, but the sun's warmth draws me at times to the shoreline.

I start to think about fish. If I could catch a fish, I could make some wonderful fish tacos with my tortilla mix and the succulent meat. I had not noticed any fish, so now I wonder if this river has fish! I will study the waters more thoroughly when it becomes less murky.

I need to make some tortillas. My hunger is overcoming my desire to quickly distance myself from the woman and move up the river. I need to find a nice camp spot and spend some time there preparing food. As I am walking, I notice the river is becoming clearer. I can see rocks at the bottom of certain spots as I walk past.

The trees are closer together here. I stop to listen. Only birds. I venture further into the trees. The ground is covered with plants. I keep wandering through the trees until I come to an open area. The sun is bright here and it gives a wonderful glow to the ground. In the middle of this bright area is a tree which appears different from the rest. I can climb the branches of this tree! I climb up a few limbs and sit. I just want to take it all in for a moment. As I look around the area from my perch, it appears untouched.

It is not until my focus moves closer that I notice the purple and green fruit dangling around me. "*¡Higos!*" I exclaim, almost falling from my branch from surprise. This Ficus Carica (Sosa Carillo) fig tree will likely save me from going hungry! I pull at a fig and it separates easily from the stem. It is ripe and pop it in my mouth. The sweetness is overwhelming. *Es como una mezcla de fresa y melocotón -* like a mix of strawberry and peach!

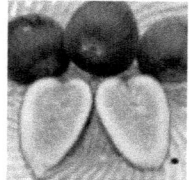

After eating several figs, I realize I should stop before I become ill. I begin to make two piles of the fig on the ground below me. One pile is ripe fig, which are darker in color. The other, the green fig, is difficult to pull from the branch. The unripened figs I will wrap and place in my pack. The ripened figs I will make into meals for the near future.

CHAPTER 6

HOME FOR NOW

I look around and realize this will be my camp. I will set up near this tree but deeper into the woods, where the plants can cover me and the trees will provide places to hide. I scout the area, in search of the perfect spot. I find a fallen cottonwood tree. It has several branches which have cemented into the ground. With some large leaves, I can make a good shelter using this frame.

I can make a fire in a small clearing that is surrounded by bushes. I hope the bushes will hide my fire. I think   I will not make a fire at night yet, because of the woman. I wonder about the best time to make a fire. In the daytime my smoke can be seen. Perhaps at dusk I can make a fire for a short while and then put it out as the evening becomes night.

It is still afternoon, so I will gather what I need to make my shelter and future fires. First though, I retrieve my two piles of figs. I place one pile near where the fire will be. The other pile I place in my shelter, where later I will work to wrap them for my pack.

I first set out to look for leaves. Anything green and large. As I gather the leaves, I try to imagine ways for me to tie them together or to make them into a roof. As I bring them back to the fallen log, I think about adding sticks to provide a place for the leaves to be caught. I like this idea because I also have to gather sticks for the fire. As I gather the sticks, I place those in two piles as well. The greener ones I lay in a pile near my fallen tree. The drier more brittle ones I place near my ripe figs at the fire spot.

As I venture further out, I gather whatever presents itself to bring back to the campsite. As I find large leaves, I gather them and race back to the shelter. These I drop into a pile until I can determine how to best use them as cover.

It is now dusk so I survey my work. My pile of brittle sticks is smaller than the greener pile, but I can gather more of those sticks in the morning. I will work on my shelter now before I can no longer see. I place the branches over my main log branches. I place them in a weave pattern so they cross each other. I use some of the leafy branches I found to make a false doorway which hangs down from the roof.

Once I make a thick layer of sticks, I begin to add handfuls of leaves. I have an epiphany as I am doing this. I will layer another weave of sticks on top of the leaves to hold them into place. I am pleased with this new thought. I can now barely see, so I stop my work and make my way over to the pile of ripe figs. These I cover with a layer of fig leaves I had apportioned for wrapping the unripened figs.

I pop a few more figs into my mouth and savor them after my hard work. Then I crawl into my new home. My pack is already snugly fit into its recesses. Tomorrow I have much to do. I will relax now and think about what I will do the following day. I pull out one of the figs from my pocket. I place it near me in case the white rabbit comes for a visit.

As the sun rises, a glimmer reaches my eyelids and my eyes pop open. I have so much to do! I carefully peer out to see what my encampment looks like in the morning light. Nothing appears to be touched and I feel a sigh of relief leave my lips. My mind has been racing all night. I think of the packet containing hooks and clear thread. I think of sticks that need to be gathered. And leaves. I think about scouting and making sure more people aren't around and searching for me.

First I look at my shelter. It needs to look like it is not my home but like it belongs here. I will add leafy branches trail off to the sides. Hopefully it will blend in. I set off to find more leafy branches. Once my pile is sufficient, I set out to find more firewood. I will also need smaller logs to keep a fire going, if I want to keep one going for heat. Once

I gather a large pile of dry wood, I notice it is getting warmer. I head to the river to gather water. I will need to find a way to hold water in larger quantities.

At the water's edge, I sit and put my feet in. I stare out at its tranquil flow and I feel happy. It is a sunshiny day and the sounds are peaceful. I feel content. I know I still have many things I want to accomplish before the day ends, but taking this time feels good. I pray, thanking God for the white rabbit, for the *higo*, and for my home.

There is something over in the reeds which glistens in the sunlight. I walk over to investigate. What I find makes me laugh out loud! A large plastic bottle is there floating, trapped by the slender grasses. I fill it and empty it several times to clean it out. Then I take the full bottle back to my camp.

I pull out my stones from the pack and set up a work area to make the flour and *mezcla* for my tortillas. I also set out the seeds to make the oil. I need to be careful not to lose the oil to the stone. I realize I should mash the seeds in my metal pot, so the oil will be there when I heat the dough.

I want to heat my water, and I want to cook the *tortillas*, but I also want to be cautious. If my fire can be made with very little smoke, I can do it without notice. If it should smoke heavily, I might have trouble. Fire is a valuable resource. If I can keep a low fire at all times, like *mi mamá* does, I won't waste the valuable fire-making resources I have. My life seems to be about taking chances. I need boiled water; I need to heat food (especially if I find a place to fish), and I may need heat for warmth in the future. I cannot allow fear to dictate over common sense. I will gather the rest of what I need to make my fire pit.

I am back on the shore, looking for stones. If I can find a nice flat one, I can also have a baking stone. For now, I will be content to find the stones to line my pit. I gather as many stones as I can carry and make my way back. The smaller stones I place in the hole I have dug. As I find larger stones, I make a ring around the hole with them. I drag a really large stone and place it near the ring. I will sit on this stone.

I make a small tower of twigs in the center of the hole. Then I make the larger sticks stand around it by placing them against each other on all sides. I place a few small logs to the side, ready to be added once the fire has taken and really burns. I light the fire using the *magnesio y cuchillo* from my pack. My pocket knife makes sparks as it hits my magnesium stick. The dried leaves and small twigs catch fire after several attempts. I cup my hands and blow on the flame.

The fire is burning clean and with very little smoke. I pull out my metal pot and heat some of the water. Each time I heat the water to a boil, I pour it into my drinking bottle. Once it is full, I use it to mix with the flour on the flat stone. As the flour moistens into dough, I roll it into balls that I will flatten to make the tortillas. I have never made a tortilla with this flour and I wonder about adding the fig to the dough. I have never made a tortilla with fig either! I start with just the flour, water and oil from the seeds to make a simple tortilla.

I put my other metal pot (the one with the mashed seeds) over the fire to heat the oil. Once it is hot, I scrape out the seed pods with a stick, leaving mostly oil. Then I put the balls of dough into the heated oil. I roll them around in it. I knead them again, allowing the oil to permeate the entire ball of dough. I place the flat stone into the fire to see if I can use it to heat the tortillas. I keep adding balls to the oil, and then once I have mixed the oil in the dough, place the new balls to the side, ready to be flattened into tortillas.

The stone is steaming in the fire, so I take a ball of dough and begin to flatten it with my palms, as I have seen my mother do a thousand times. I keep patting it back and forth until it is a flat circle of dough. I place it on the stone and it makes a sizzle. Quickly I pick it up and turn it over. I count to ten and turn it. I do this over and over until it seems cooked throughout. Then I stack it on another flat stone. Once I have a nice stack of tortillas, I repackage the flour and put it into my pack. I roll several of the tortillas together and wrap each of those rolls in the corn husks I kept from my tamales. These I also place back into my pack. Along with my green figs, my pack contains an abundance of food now.

I grab a tortilla from the pile and eat it. It is slightly bitter but tastes good. I go to the pile of figs and take one, wrap it in another tortilla and take a bite. It is really good! I eat several and realize I feel full! I haven't felt full in a long time. I am proud of my labors. I think of how proud my parents would be, and then a somber mood overtakes me.

I stoke the fire and begin boiling water again. Once my drinking bottle is full, I refill the bottle I found. If I could find another, I could make one of the bottles full of the boiled water. All in good time. God has been providing and so I will take it as it comes. I crouch at the water's edge and begin filling my bottle. I look around the river. I see the shadow of a fish go by. Then another. It is a school of fish! The thought of fried fish in my diet is dizzying. I will be up at dawn.

When I get back to my camp I mound my rocks closer to the burning embers. I add a small log. I want the fire to burn through the night, but I also want to keep the fire's glow to a minimum. I sit by the fire as dusk sets in. I am stringing the hooks from my packet. I will use two of them. Maybe with two lines, I will catch a fish! Once my fire is safely packed and my campground is cleaned up, I crawl into my shelter. I fall asleep with a satisfaction I feel deep within *mi pecho*. I cross my arms over my chest, as if to protect that feeling, and fall asleep quickly.

CHAPTER 7

FISHERMAN

For my breakfast I roll up my tortilla with a fig inside, mashing it carefully. I finish it quickly and make another. Then I take my walking stick, my pack and my fishing lines and head for the river. It is barely dawn. I pick some bagworms as I pass by the cottonwood near my path. As I prick the bag with my hook, the end of a worm wriggles out the other side. "That will get their attention!" I think to myself.

I toss my lines into the water, carefully tying each beneath a knob on my walking stick. I pull out some beans to munch as I patiently wait. My mind wanders and I begin to think of ways to make this river useful to me. The thought occurs to me to make a raft! I can make it during these long periods while trying to catch fish. I find a forked stick and prop my walking stick into it. I will not venture far from my fishing spot, but I can search nearby for what I might need.

The willow tree will provide good straps for the raft. The reeds along the shoreline will too. I will need some sturdy logs that will float and are not too rotted or dry. These will be my biggest challenge, so I save log hunting for last. I gather reeds and willow branches into piles near my walking stick. The willow branches seem more like *látigos* than branches, so I test the whipping power of one of them. I hear the air currents whisk past my ears as I raise it and lower it quickly. Its end makes a snapping sound just before it falls limply to the ground.

My grin fades as I see my walking stick bending dangerously close to the water. I run to grab it! Just in the nick of time, I pull back on the stick and feel the tension. It could just be another stick or water plant, but it could be a fish! I step back carefully, gently tugging at the line. I could hear my father's voice telling me not to pull too hard. *"No estiras rápido - más despacito mijo"*, his voice tells me sternly. Slowly I tug at the line, then let it go a little, then tug again. I begin to feel something give. Though it is coming in more quickly, the line is not lax, so I don't believe I have lost whatever I have hooked. I look for something to wind my line since I am having to back up near the trees. I grab a short but stout stick and begin winding my line as quickly as I can. I will need to use this in the future because I am wasting precious time. I continue to pull on the line and back toward the woods, and suddenly something silver shines on the shore. It flops back and forth and I know I have caught my first fish! I keep holding the line taut as I move toward the fish. I grab the portion of the line nearest the mouth and pull him up into the air, near my face. *¡Hola Señor Pescado! ¡Lo bonito de tu parte venir a cenar!* I tell him in my most formal voice. I do believe it is nice of this fish to come to dinner.

I will have to come back later for my raft building collections. Right now I have a fish to clean and fry! As I lay the fish on my flat stone, I wish I had the knife I had seen *mi mamá* use to chop off the fish head. The fish squirms as I prepare to open my pocket knife with one hand. Thankfully it is sharp and it is not as hard to get the head off as I thought it would be. Then I take off the tail fin. I make a slit up the belly and peel back the sides. There is the spine, and carefully I extract this from one end to the other. The pale thin bones come out easily with this motion. I put another small log on the fire and stoke it with a stick which is there for that purpose. I realize while looking at this stick that I have begun to accumulate many possessions!

I crush some more sunflower seeds at the bottom of my metal pot and set it on the fire. When I hear it sizzle I place the fish, its halves held together by its skin, into the pan. The sound is like heaven. I leave the fish skin face up, since I will peel it off once the fish has cooked. I move the pot to the edge of the fire so my fish can cook slowly. I do not want to burn it! I check my pack for seasoning. There is *polvo de chile* in one of the packets! I am grateful that so many food spices are used to cure people. I do not use much, but sprinkle a little of the chili powder into the oil around the fish.

I am uncertain how long I need to cook fish so I will do it by scent. I use a forked stick to pull my pot out of the fire.

It smells delicious! I gently pull the skin off the fish. The meat is white and flaky and steaming. I can hardly contain my excitement. I search my pack for a spoon. I carefully scoop a piece of fish and whisper a short prayer. I savor the morsel and chew it carefully, wanting to make each bite last. It does not take me long to consume the fish, as it was a small one.

I make the short trek to the river to clean my pot, spoon and stone. I have used my oil cloth to clean my pocket knife, as has been my habit since it was given to me on my fourth birthday. I have great respect for the dangers of a sharp knife, but even greater respect for its usefulness. I carefully put my wares back into my pack. Back at the campsite, I once again shore up the sides around the fire and make it smaller and less obvious.

I will wait for dusk to cast another line. My father always said early morning or early evening were the fishing times. In the meantime I will gather and sort the supplies to make my raft. I set out in search of branches to make the frame of the raft. By late afternoon, I have found only three logs that can be used. I did find more logs which are suitable for firewood, so these I stack between two trees and cover with leaves. I decide to make my raft at the base of the fig tree. That way, I can eat fresh figs while I work. I have my reeds, willow branches and three branches laid out, so I begin to work. Soon I realize I can use smaller branches to weave between the larger ones, so I gather several of those. I strip the smaller twigs from the branches and smooth out the bark with a small stone. I use the willow branches as twine and tie them off frequently. I use the reeds to tie alternating sections together. I do not know which of the knots or ties will hold, so I determine I will make many of them. The sun is hot but the shade keeps me comfortable as I work. My hands tire and it is getting late in the day. I finish my work for the day by gathering some sap from a nearby cottonwood. This I smear over the knots of both the willow and the reed. I will check this tomorrow to see if it hardens.

I grab my walking stick from behind a tree at the camp and set off for the river once again. From my sack I pull the stick with the fishing line wound around it and begin to prepare my walking stick. I have to look around for the worms, which I had placed under a stone to keep them moist. I cast my line out and sit to wait. The air is pleasant. The sunlight is flickering on the water. I can hear the birds gathering in their night branches, the songs filling the air. This is a time of great peace and I understand why my father loves fishing.

CHAPTER 8

STORMS

By dark I have not caught a fish, so I wind my line once again and pack up my belongings. I make my way to camp. I am thinking the mornings are an easier time to fish, and evenings will be better for raft building. With this plan in mind I reach the camp, barely able to make out the opening of my shelter. I climb inside and reflect on the victories of the day. As I drift off to sleep, I think about swimming in the river. I haven't bathed or washed my clothes in a few days.

I awaken with the dawn, and gather my pack and walking stick. I will fish for a few hours and make my raft for the remainder of the day. I pull out both lines for today's fishing. I search for another stubby stick on which to wind the second fishing line. As the sun is rising, I am eating fig and tortillas with my fishing lines already in the stream. I feel good about today. It is already beginning to get warm. I guess I will swim in the late morning, after I finish fishing in a few hours.

I feel a tug on my pole, and I am happy I haven't been distracted or wandered off this time. I stand to get a better grip on the pole. I wish I had two poles in order to leave my other line in the water. Since it is not the case, I shrug to myself and begin to slowly pull on the stick and walk backward. I start to wind the taut line onto its stick. Suddenly the other line is taut as well! Oh my! I begin to wind the other line as well, alternating between the two lines. Since the winding is slow anyway, I concentrate on doing this for a while and then begin to walk backward, pulling both lines simultaneously. Furiously I wind them both again. I keep repeating this workout until I see two silver pieces, moving on the shore. I gather them up, walking to my camp with a spring in my step.

I don't know how to smoke fish to keep it for a longer time but I will prepare both fish and try to wrap the cooked fish I can't eat to save for later. I know I don't want to get sick, so I won't be able to save it for long. It takes longer to make two fish ready and to cook them since my pot will not hold them both. Once the first fish is cooked, I sit to eat it. Then I cook the second one. I peel off its skin and place a tortilla over the top of it, leaving it in the pot. I put the whole thing inside a large leaf and carry it all with me to the fig tree. I work there for the afternoon, weaving and tying. The three logs look ornate with all the lattice work. It is not very wide but it is long enough for me to lie on it. Of course I would roll off of it on either side if I tried to use it!

The sap seems to be drying nicely on the spots where I have applied it, so I add more of to the knots and then to the other parts of the raft as well. I clean up the area, and place my pot of fish carefully at the top of my pack. I will find more logs to widen the raft. I head off deeper into the woods for my search. I pull out my compass because the sun is obscured as I travel deeper through the foliage. I find some branches which will serve well as crosshatch to the larger logs. That will make it wider but not as strong as I would like. I drag several of these behind me as I make my way back to the fig tree. I lace and tie for the remainder of the afternoon. When the day begins to wane, I open my pack to eat the other fish. The fig eaten with the fish is delicious. I have never had a fish taco like this before!

Tomorrow after fishing, I will test the raft. I will get my bathing, washing and testing all done at once. I smile at the thought of this efficiency. I will add some extra straps to my raft, in case I need to strap myself on. I am not sure it will work, but the idea of straps appeals to me. I begin tying long pieces of willow to various parts of the raft, making a coil out of each strap. I use a reed tie to fasten each coil to its segment of the raft. I gather sap and apply it to the willow ties just as nightfall approaches.

The morning has an orange glow to it. I stretch and look around, eager to find what has changed. I put on my pack, pick up my walking stick, and make my way to the river. There seems to be a storm brewing, because the sky is darkening quickly and the air is muggy with moisture. I opt to test my raft quickly, and delay fishing until tomorrow. The water is still calm when I approach, carrying my raft overhead. I set it down in the water and wade out into the river with it. It floats! I try to climb on it but I think it will crack the branches on my side, so I back off and push it along instead. After spending several minutes floating, I decide the storm will hit anytime now. I kick the water with my feet and move toward the shore.

Just as I am pulling the raft out, a light rain begins. I walk the raft back to the fig tree. I rest it up against the tree and climb into the branches. I need to replenish my stock of figs anyway, so I begin this task. *"Uno para mi boca, uno para mi bolsa"* The one-for-my-mouth-one-for-my-pack game goes on for some time. Then I just put them in the pack once I am full. I also gather some additional green figs because this weather has made me feel uneasy.

Later in the day, the sun comes out, but even with that, something feels wrong. I close my eyes as I lay back on the branches. The sun feels warm and my clothes start to dry. When my eyes pop open, I am being pelted with large drops of water. All around me the rain is coming down in torrents. The tree is protecting me from the worst of it. I see my raft below, the water starting to rise against it. It will float away! I climb down and pull it up to the branches. I climb up further and set the raft on two leafy branches which hold it nicely.

The amount of water gathering on the floor of the woods is alarming. A bright flash rips across the sky above me. Several seconds pass by and then I hear a loud crack and low rumbling. It is so loud. The torrent of rain continues. The water beneath the tree is now swirling. Within a few minutes I realize the ground beneath me has become the river! I try to remain calm, as I am feeling the panic within me rising. The tree groans as if from great weight. I instinctively uncoil one of the straps from my raft and tie it to my ankle. I see figs dropping into the water.

It occurs to me to grab the ripe figs and wrap them in leaves. As I get a bundle, I tie it onto the raft. I start to use smaller more pliable twigs to tie the bundles first. As I get groups of bundles, I use the straps to fix them to the raft. I work at this for a long time. I am drenched, scared and shaking when I stop to take a rest. I start in again, this time bundling green figs. They are less in danger of dropping off the tree but they will also last longer in my food supply if I do get swept away with this current beneath me.

The work keeps my mind off my fears, so I concentrate on the task at hand. The rains do not relent. When I have exhausted the supply of figs in my immediate reach, I stop. I don't want to risk sliding or falling out of the tree. I remain still and watch as the water rises. It has now reached just below the first branches. There is no one out here to rescue me. Monsoon season has begun. I will have to be very careful near the river from now on. Thankfully I am nestled into the tree branches and I can close my eyes. I am worn out from fear and I drift off to sleep.

There are stars above me when my eyes open. I can make out the water below and it is still dangerously high. I am too groggy to risk much movement but I see some raindrops on a leaf near me so I move it to aim at my mouth. I continue doing this from the leaves surrounding me until I feel my thirst is quenched. I don't know how long I will have to remain in this tree, but I know once the ground beneath is dry again, I will have to search for higher ground. I think of my large water bottle. I am sure it has been swept away, unless my shelter has retained it somehow. I will need a bottle like that if I venture away from the river.

CHAPTER 9

TRAPPED

The next day is hot and passes slowly. The water might be receding but it is difficult to tell. The current is passing under the tree so no markings remain on the trunk below. I am slowly eating a fig when I realize I have nowhere to relieve myself. I really have to go! I might feel bad about what I am about to do, but then I realize that all I had done in all the days before, in completely good conscience, was now floating down the same river. I am learning to be rather creative in my youth, and learning to improvise.

Sitting in this tree, I try to create a game, so I can keep my mind occupied. I try to remember herbs my mother taught me about and what they are used for. I try to think of their leaves and where they are found. I have yet to fully inventory what my mother has packed for me. I suppose I should have, but I had a lot to do! I can't think of it now, as I would never risk taking the pack off my back. I take my mother's advice very seriously. She has earned the respect of our entire village and has cured many people. Many of those people have come back to her over the years, bearing gifts from their farms and businesses, to thank her for something she did for them in the past. My mother rarely charges for her medical services. She relies on good will and sometimes asks favors in return. She might say, "Yes, I set your leg and now you have a pain reliever which will last you many weeks." Then she would say, "If you someday pass by such-and-such riverbed and find such-and-so looking plant, please bring me as much of it as you can carry. That will be payment enough for me".

Over the years, her stock of dried herbs was the envy of all the *curanderas* for miles. She would trade some of her special herbs for curing recipes or some ancient knowledge a certain family was known to pass on. She would cure other *curanderas* when their knowledge did not cover their own ailments. She would invite doctors from other countries to our home and, in exchange for teachings about injectables and purification methods, she would give them potent medicines for problems they described but could not fix. Given that many of the doctors came back over the years, I suspect many of her cures worked miracles, just as our people had experienced.

Elena will be our family *curandera* now, but my mother passed on her extensive knowledge to me in case she had no more children. It had taken her many years from my birth to have another child. My father tried to discourage my training in what I had been taught by my mother (woman's work), and he gave me instruction on many farming and survival skills. From when I was a very young age, each of them sought to impart all the knowledge they had so our family secrets and techniques would continue. I can remember barely walking, and I remember bending over to examine plants at the very same time. My mother told me I walked at six months old and she proudly states I was learning herbs and habitat even earlier than that!

I learned to use a bow and arrow as soon as I could walk steadily and would follow my father into the desert surrounding our pueblo. I learned bird calls and how to hide myself. I learned how to farm, and how to irrigate, and how to salvage something from disaster. I miss that. I miss my father. I am shaking now, tears pouring down my cheeks. I don't know what happened back there, after we had crossed the border. It seems so long ago. I resolve now to go back there when I am a man, and find them. I will find my parents or find out what happened to them. I feel numb as my body slips into a deep sleep. This tree is like God's hand, holding me gently and safely.

The sun is out again. It is hot and I can see the ground now, under the water below. It looks shallow enough, but I doubt I will risk it. I don't know if the mud is thick and if I will sink. I am still afraid. I eat some more figs, grateful for their abundance. I carefully sip from the water bottle I finally had to pull from my pack. I kept the bottle out and stuffed it down the front of my shirt, because I wanted to risk no further disturbances of my pack. I figure if it rains again, I can hold it out to collect water. I say a prayer and ask God to hold back on the rain, at least until the ground below me dries and I can find safety on higher ground.

I hear people. I hear laughter and someone yelling. I feel every part of my being stiffen in fear. I can pinpoint the direction to the river, the main part. I think it is ironic I am now part of the river. I peer out and try to find the noise. Suddenly there is a blue raft. It is not far from me. Orange-vested people are sitting in it, using paddles. They are hooting and hollering loudly as they have near misses with tree branches. They are drifting rapidly, so the river must be moving fast. As they near my vantage, still in the distance though, I press my body against the tree. Am I wearing anything which will attract attention? I look down at my clothing. My mother had dressed me for our trip. My clothing is black or olive green. My pack is olive green. I am relieved.

The raft passes by and I pray for them and for their safety. Even in a raft of such a large size, the river looks dangerous by comparison. I wonder if I will ever make it out of this tree. I wonder if I will be able to drink the muddy water beneath me. Then I think of this tree with my safe and comfortable spot, and the figs with their sweetness not only filling me but their juiciness obviously giving me water, and with renewed tears running down my cheeks, I thank God for his provision and tell him I am sorry for my doubts.

I have begun to use the tree again. I am gathering its twigs and tying them to make ropes. I am weaving strings of tied twigs with other strings to make them stronger. It is a long and tedious process. Waiting in a tree for epic waters to subside is a long and tedious process, so I figure my industry has merit. I do beg the tree for forgiveness, but I also feel it understands. I begin to see progress when I realize how long my rope is, and how thick! I try with all my might to pull it apart. I do this down its entire length. I keep adding to it and after I add considerable length, I try to pull it apart again. I wish I could get to the sap and apply it. I think it gives a resilience and strength to the straps, and so I want to give that to the rope.

I have wrapped so many bundles of figs to the raft that I wonder if I have taken the whole tree. I look up and see the figs hanging there. Not even close! I sigh with contentment and eat a few. I have to keep changing my tasks to keep from dying of boredom because the days linger on.

The ground is now a pattern of cracked patchy clay underneath the tree. I resolve to lower my body from the branch above it and test it. It moves beneath my toe pressing it. I try to place my foot on it. It only sinks an inch or so. Now I am on the ground, with both feet. Can I walk? I make steps and yes, I can move without sinking into the earth. I walk back to the tree. I pat its trunk and whisper my thanks and good-byes, while pulling my raft from its branches. I will gather what I can, and float it along with me on my raft. At the next sign of rain, however, I will need to grab what is most important and run for higher ground.

Riparian Regions - Babocomari

CHAPTER 10

RABBITS AND RATTLERS

I carry my raft overhead to my former campsite. It looks nothing like the home I had made. I see the tree limb and log is still intact. I can see inside because all of my leaves and branches have been washed away. However, there in the mud is my bottle! I am overjoyed! I carefully go in and pull the bottle from its wedged position. It is still full of water from when I had last filled it with boiled water. Amazing. I take this and my raft to the water's edge and once the raft is afloat, I secure the water bottle to the raft and begin walking downstream. As I pull my raft along, I can feel it drifts easily with my steps. I have secured a long rope to it in several places and I allow it to drift out from the bank to ensure easier travel. I have a plan. I will stop along the way to gather beans and sunflowers as I find them. I will need to replenish my stock and the raft will carry far more than my pack. When I find large leaves, I examine them to make sure they are not poisonous. Once I determine they are useful, I place them on the raft. I will need them to wrap the seeds or beans I gather as I travel.

I want to cross the river, mostly because I miss the white rabbit. I have found abundance on this side, but I still wonder about my friend and I still have a desire to find out if he is okay.

I tie my raft to the trees and scour the woods looking for beans or sunflowers. I have found a few bean trees and my raft is beginning to fill. I try to find the wood's edge to see if sunflowers abide there, but still I do not find them. On one expedition, I follow my compass due west, and there before me is a jojoba bush. Jojoba is a natural fungicide and an oil which does not go rancid quickly. I gather its seeds. It is not known for its food qualities but I know I can use its oils to cook food. Given my lack of sunflower seed, I am grateful for this one.

I think about the cactus that loom before me in the desert landscape. Before the monsoons, the jojoba seed were ripening and now during the monsoon season, the prickly pear will soon ripen. The desert is where I can collect these valuable foods for my oils and meals. I can dry the prickly pear with the sun, and grind and melt the jojoba for my oils.

Walking back toward the river, I think of how much will change if I no longer have a water source. I won't be able to clean myself, or gather fresh water, but then I also won't get washed downstream or be stuck in a tree. I had been truly terrified during the flood, so I continue to ponder my options as I walk along. Something off to the side catches my attention. It is a building of some sort. A very large tree stands near it. There is not much vegetation to hide in, so I must be careful. I creep along carefully, trying to get a better look. It is well kept but I don't see anyone near it. I creep up to a board. It has writing which I can't read. I can read most of "San Pedro House". *"San Pedro",* I repeat to myself. I move back toward the river, trying to crouch low to the ground.

The San Pedro House Tree

My eyes are now widened with fear. The sound is unmistakable. Nearby I hear its rattle. Very slowly I move my head to try and locate the snake. It is very close and it is poised to strike. Fear is melting my heart. Suddenly something white rushes past the snake's head. It then darts to the side, as if taunting. The snake snaps its open mouth in that direction now and slithers quickly away from me. It is chasing a white rabbit!

I pray fervently for the safety of the rabbit as I run toward the river, hoping I don't encounter any more danger. Just as I approach the spot where I have hidden my raft, I hear voices in the distance. This area is much more inhabited than where I had made my home. I am not safe here! Quickly I pull the raft back into the water and gently guide it along. The water is more shallow now and the river much more narrow, which I had not noticed until now. Thankfully, the river is still swollen from the rains or this area might not have accommodated my raft well. I still have not seen any people, but someone could be watching me. I keep my eyes ahead, making my way down the simple path which lines the river.

A bridge overhead has just come into view. The sound of a motor makes me jump. It is as though the whole area has come alive and decided to announce itself to me! It is still early in the day and this is fortunate because I can see I am about to bathe shortly. I can either travel in the river and pass under the bridge, or climb its steep banks and go up and over its road to the other side. A second motor sound makes my decision for me. I wade into the water and float along with the current.

I feel less exposed now, with only my face out of the water. Occasionally, my raft drifts beside me as if in a race. I need to look for a good spot to camp early since I want my clothing to dry. I also want to remain in the water, drifting further away from the bridge. I keep floating for now and survey the raft as it again approaches my view.

I drift lazily along, occasionally closing my eyes to enjoy the sun on my face. I had missed this method of river travel from my first visit to this river. A long shadow covers my eyes so I open them. I am passing under another bridge! I hear no motors so my panic subsides immediately. The flow of the river is strong but not overwhelming. My feet are pointed north (or as northward as a winding river allows!) and I feel at peace.

A gust of wind blows hard against my face. I see only blue sky above me so I don't worry much about it. When the rain begins to sprinkle on my face, my concern grows remarkably. Such a perfect day! Why is there rain? The sky above me is now turning black. I wade to the shore's edge and pull my raft onto it.

I have to get to higher ground now! The raft is heavier for the water but it is still bearable for me. I lift it up and move slowly up the sides of the bank. The banks here are not steep and I whisper a quick *"Gracias a Dios"* and continue making my way toward the trees. As I walk under the canopy of a small grove of trees, the rains are pouring down all around. I will not be able to make a fire as the entire area is saturated and this rain has only just begun. I am not far enough away from the river to be able to sleep so I sit and think about my situation. I can try to make my raft smaller by cutting it to a smaller size and using it as a frame. I can strap the frame to my back using the willow branches. The leaves can cover the bundles, and I can tie those down using the remaining branches. I am glad I secured so many coils of willow to the raft. As I saw the branches to a smaller size with my pocket knife, I try to think of a new plan. I determine I will travel west from here, toward the desert.

The rains stop as abruptly as they started, and there is a glow from the setting sun. The water from the river has not reached my spot, so sleeping here is now possible. I can secure my wrist to the raft just in case. It will be harder to float on the raft now that it is small, but it will still float I am sure. I shiver as the night air touches my wet clothing. I curl up tightly and use a bundle as my pillow. Sleep does not elude me because I am exhausted.

With the rising sun I do not lose my desire to distance myself from the river, so I put my pack on my front side and hoist the frame to my back. There are so many loops of willow it makes for a thick strap on either side, and the frame easily stays on my back. One of the main logs on the raft bumps the back of my calf as I walk, but I will make a decision about it later. For now I have my provisions and I will seek safety.

I walk along trying to keep my course due west. I walk for a long time. Eventually I come to a fence of barbed wire. I know I must get away from this place. A sign is posted on the fence, and I can only read a few words near its ending:

WARNING
U.S. ARMY INSTALLATION
NO TRESPASSING
AVISO
NO TRESPASAR
BASE MILITAR U.S. ARMY

I can no longer head due west and I am concerned if I follow a military fence line, someone will encounter me here. I turn back to some trees and follow the line to the north. I don't wish to be seen. I walk along and notice trees are green to the west of where I am walking. I take out my father's compass to make sure. They are due west of my position so I walk there.

As I hike along, the sun is directly overhead and the day is clear. The sun makes my mood hopeful, even though it is hot. There is one thing I had not been considering during the afternoon rains: how to collect the waters so I can drink without having a river nearby. I keep my course toward the trees ahead, searching around me for any signs of life. So far as I am aware, I am the only person out here. I am happy for this.

When the clouds gather I notice immediately. I hope I can reach the trees before the next deluge. Although I am very hot from my walk, I am not looking forward to the rain. I do want to figure out how to capture the rainwater so I will not be without water on my journey through the desert. It seems a conflict of desires. I walk along thinking of possible funnels to use even as the torrents of rain pelt me. I find my worry of finding water after entering the desert ironic considering the magnitude and frequency of the waters currently falling upon me.

The trees give me some cover overhead from the rain which is coming down in sheets. I am drenched. I have not been traveling more than a couple of hours and there before me is a river. I know it is not the San Pedro, because I have used the compass this time. I survey the river before me, smaller than the previous one but swollen nonetheless. I realize I could float and not walk and that would make my calf feel better in the long run. Upon closer inspection though, the river is running back toward the San Pedro! There will be no making a fire given the weather, so I decide to walk the shoreline against the current and continue my trek west. The clouds are so dark I don't know the time of day now. I know it is not yet night, but it appears to be dusk as I walk along. The longer I watch the river, the more objects I begin to notice floating along past me. A gas can that bobs near the shoreline is quickly plucked. There are objects floating past me which make me wonder if I am not witnessing part of a grand flood; one that is whisking possessions away as it gathers water from this storm.

As it gets darker, I try to move to an area away from the river swell and toward what might even be a path. Even in this darkness I can see the river has widened. The rains continue and I might as well walk as far as I am able. There will be nowhere to sleep tonight. I am bracing my mind with determination for the upcoming all-nighter, when I come upon clearing. The picnic bench here before me would not normally be an option, but it draws me like a strong magnet and I realize I am now curled up on it. I pray for sunshine in the morning. I am cold but somehow I feel a warmth finding this spot and fall fast asleep.

CHAPTER 11

IN THE NEWS

"Mommy, it is Gabriel! I recognize him from Naco! His family died in that terrible fire!" A young girl's voice wakes me with a start. There beside me are two women and a girl around my age. The sad look on her face as she gazes at me causes me to reflect it back. "See, Mommy! It is him!" she exclaims excitedly. I smile at her excitement and she smiles back. The sun is warm and I am happy. I am also afraid of these people. Slowly I stand and straighten my pack. I reach for my frame. "We will take him to Social Services," one of the women starts to say to the other. As she turns to discuss it further, a white rabbit bursts past all of us, barreling toward the river. It is my *conejo blanco*! I can tell by the remaining green leaf on his leg! I grab my frame and run after him with all my might. From the shouts behind me, I can tell this is unacceptable to the ladies I leave behind. As soon as I reach the bank I make a quick decision: jump!

I am now floating back to the place I had just left! The people will come to look for me here. I can still hear them shouting. I see the white rabbit on the opposite shore now. I wonder for a moment how he got there. Rather than think about it further, I stand up and race up the bank to find him. He is running out to a field and back toward the west. With the morning sun behind me, I feel the warmth on my back. Here and there I catch a glimpse of white fur. I take out my compass to get my bearings. I am heading northwest. It pleases me that my rabbit has led me in the direction I need to go. I will need to travel far, because people know I am here now.

The day is hot, which dries my clothing and takes away my inner chills, but as it continues I feel my thirst. I drink some of my precious bottle. I have two filled for this unknown visit to the desert. I know I must be careful, since I don't know where my next water fill will be. I grab some of the pods from my supplies and chew the moisture from them. This makes me feel better and stronger. I keep a good pace and look all around for the rabbit. The sky to the southwest is growing dark. It is much too soon for nightfall! I focus on moving as quickly as I can. Whatever the tall weeds are in this field, I am thankful they make my trek undetectable.

The rain begins to fall, slowly at first and then with a large howl from the wind, sheets of rain fall on me. At first it feels like warm water, and I trudge through the fields comfortably. It isn't until later that I feel my body begin to tremble with cold. I know I can't stay out in this rain all night long. I pull myself along, praying for somewhere to take shelter, even a bush. Just as I feel I might fall where I am, I see a large dark object ahead. It is a barn! A small light gleams from a door at one side. I stumble across the muddy yard, sliding some and hoping I won't fall. The door opens easily and the lamp gives the inside a dim light. I memorize where the ladder to the hayloft is and shut the door behind me. Creeping up the ladder, I make as little noise as I can. I do not want to disturb any animals and call attention to this barn. I cover my frame with pieces of straw and then find another spot to settle in, covering myself the best I can before drifting quickly to sleep.

When I wake up I can see it is already very late. The barn doors are open. I will have to be very careful. I wish I could stay up here for a long time but I know I have not gone far enough for a long rest. I attach the frame to my back and carefully climb down the ladder. When I reach the barn floor I am face to face with a boy who is younger than me! "*Shhhh*," I put my finger to my mouth to indicate I want this to be our secret. He smiles but then he runs toward the house! I feel panic in my belly and I feel sick. I start to heave right there. Nothing comes out but the motion is uncontrollable. I have to run! I have to leave! Instead, I am holding my stomach bent over a pile of straw. The boy is there again. He smiles and hands me a loaf of bread and an apple. He then presses his finger to his lips. "*Shhh*," is all he says as well. He then peeks out the doorway and then motions for me to come. He points to some trees not far off the back of the barn. I smile and wave my thanks. My mother told me to never speak, no matter the circumstance, and I trust her judgment. I go toward the some bushes and old vehicles off the back of the barn as quickly as I can, afraid of being discovered at any moment.

What I do not know is already today I have become a local

celebrity. The Sierra Vista Herald has reported that one Gabriel Martinez, sole survivor of a fire which took his entire family in Naco, Arizona, was seen by the Babocomari River. The article has details how many people thought Gabriel had perished in the fire but no remains had been found. It states that witnesses report him to be disoriented but appearing to be in good health. This is their first lead. A mystery to be solved! In this small close-knit area, it is sure to inspire a search for the missing boy. Even as the farmer and his family sit down to pray for their evening meal, I do not realize just how close I am to being found out. As the father finishes a satisfying meal and pulls out his newspaper, he begins to read aloud about the missing boy. His son squirms in his seat while his mother tries to calm him so he doesn't interrupt his father. Once his father finishes the story, the son blurts out, "I saw that boy today. He was in our barn!" The father, understanding the gravity of the runaway youth's situation, makes a call to the sheriff and to the newspaper reporter who wrote the article.

It is daylight and there is almost nowhere to hide. The rains have caused a few grasses to rise quickly but I can see there is little that is forgiving in this terrain. I pull out my compass to get my bearings, and just as I start on my northwesterly path, the sound of a motor causes me to freeze in my tracks. Crouching behind a meager bush, I can see a passing truck. There is a road near me! This will not do, so I set my course due west and continue walking from small shrub to tree, trying to find anything which will hide me in daylight. As I walk up and down small hills, I notice there are grasses thicker ahead. I sigh audibly in relief. It makes me realize I have not heard the sound of my own voice in a long time. The sun is very hot even though it is still morning. I need to stop and drink. I still feel comfortable inside because of the bread and apple given to me. As I ponder the generosity, a light crack causes my eyes to widen. I stop and try to crouch low to the ground. I look around, trying to see what is here with me. Another crackle and crunch nearby makes my stomach feel queasy. "*Lo majestad*" I whisper to myself. The majesty of what is before me takes my breath away. A tall pronghorn walks beside me, its white backside toward me. It turns its head toward me. The white rings of its neck seem perfect, like a necklace draped in various lengths. Its small black antlers are like a crown on its head. It regards me lightly and then continues to graze. I am breathless. I am in awe. Already on my knees, I say a prayer of protection for both this pronghorn and myself. When I look up, it is gone. Gradually I rise to my feet and begin my trek again.

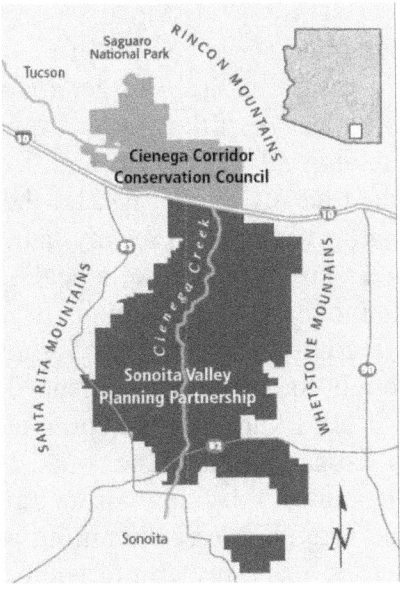

Riparian Regions - Ciénega Creek

CHAPTER 12

MONSOONS

The sun is directly overhead when I come upon a dirt road. I am wary as I choose to cross it. I stop at a yucca plant on the other side, listening and surveying the area. Realizing I am standing next to a great treasure, I forget about the road and begin to gather the leaves of the yucca. I quickly strap them to my frame, feeling my excitement build. As I walk along I think of all the uses my mother had for these leaves. Soaking its leaves will give me soap for my hair. If I get a sunburn, a scratch, or a cut, it will make a healing salve. It will reduce any inflammation and swelling. Its tea would cleanse my blood. I continue walking and soon I see a highway, close enough to see its pavement. I consider walking away from it but I know I must continue to travel west. Walking away from it will take me south. I stop near a bush and listen. No sounds. I decide to make a run for it! I climb the small bank, scramble over the railing to the road bed and then race across, using my arm to vault the railing on the other side, then slide down on a bit of loose soil. I run until I can no longer run and find a resting place beneath a Joshua tree. It is time to eat and drink. The figs are delectable and I suck the stickiness from my fingers with delight. My water is low. I will need to find water soon. I feel my eyes closing in the hot sun. A siesta is just what I need.

A prickly sensation blowing on my face wakes me with a start. All around me is darkness, but not the darkness of nightfall. I choke as I try to breathe. The air is thick with a brown dust. I duck to the ground and move my face near the base of the small tree. Coughing, I try to breathe using my sleeve. Just when I think I will die here under this tree, the dust dissipates. I look up to see a brown wall of dust swirling away. The sky lights up with a flash of lightning. It is both beautiful and frightening. I start to count. A loud clap of thunder jolts me to my feet. That made the ground tremble! I pull out the compass to get my bearings. I will head north-west. I need to find water. The granules of dust make my parched mouth feel even worse but I am afraid to spit out any moisture. The storm is roughly ten miles away. I start walking. I am afraid to walk on the hilltops, and I am afraid to walk in the valleys between them. In front of me there is no choice but to pick one of them. I choose the valley, as the lightning still has me scared. I walk along as fast as I can because I have no shelter and cannot see what is on the other side of the hills.

Another flash of lighting, as large as the previous one, lights up the darkened cloudy sky. A crack of thunder follows immediately, and before I can even think the storm is upon me and I am being drenched with rain. I open my mouth upon instinct, grateful for the downpour. I am so thirsty I can barely understand my danger. It is when I realize the water is up to my knees that I understand the valley has become a river. Quickly, I scramble up the hillside, my hands clawing at the grasses and my knees buried in mud. I continue up the slope at an angle because I am still afraid of the lightning which had hit nears its peak. Once I reach the top of the hill, I can see nothing but rivers of water surrounding me. I have nowhere to go! I sit and ponder, opening my mouth to catch the rain. I take out my empty bottles and dig a muddy holder for them in the ground. Hopefully the heavy rain will fill them. I think of my yucca leaves and remove one of them from the frame. Allowing it to get wet on all sides I begin to massage the leaf over my head. It smells heavenly, bringing back a crushing reminder of my mother shampooing my hair not so long ago. It does seem like a long time though! The rain washes the soap out almost as quickly as I can get it to lather but it all feels good anyway. I shove the long leaf into my pocket. I may want to scrub my shirt or pants with it sometime soon.

The rain is lighter now, and although the rivers of water are still there, I can see they are now less swollen. In the distance I can see the colorful sky of evening. I have to find some sort of night shelter, or at least not have to ford a stream in the dark. I walk down the hill and try to find a good place to cross. I use my compass to get my bearings. Soon it will be night and I may have to make my way using stars, if there are any out by nightfall. I cross carefully, keeping my footing, but try to trudge across quickly enough not to get stuck in the mire. I cannot afford to stop or to fall while I cross. Safely on the other side, I continue to walk the slightly hilly terrain. It makes the travel slower than normal, especially with the rain still falling. Now I travel hilltop to hilltop, trying to avoid water as I head northwest in the growing dusk. After what seems a couple of hours, I spot a larger shadow on the horizon. It looks like a treeline, but I am not sure. If it is, a larger river is likely there. It may be a blessing and a curse. I set my sights on the dark shadows in the distance, noting internally that it is a slight shift north/northwest. If I can find a tree to climb, I will be able to sleep. I begin to pay close attention to the ground under my feet as the trees come into view. Sure enough, the closer I get, the more marshy the land feels beneath me. Just ahead, a tree growing in a wild tangle of directions appears. I can climb into its branches easily, and its forks intertwine giving me a comfortable spot to recline. I smile with satisfaction as I ease back onto my frame and fall asleep, my arms clutching my pack around my stomach.

The birds have determined to wake me with the first morning light. I can see the sun creeping up and the sky is now clear. I survey my new surroundings. There is a river running north, not 100 feet from my perch. It is not rushing but it is not what I would consider lazy at this point either. I am still soaked, and the idea of a float appeals to me. I detach my frame, reverting it to its raft status. I attach its tether. I survey the water for any signs of danger and plunge in. My feet heading north, I lay on my back and allow the current to carry me. At midday I realize the water is growing sluggish, so I move toward the bank to walk for awhile. The sun is hot and I welcome the chance to dry. I walk out from the tree-lined shore and savor the hot sun while walking through the tall grasses. This feels like a sanctuary to me. I pull out one of my partially full water bottles and take a slow sip. I am unsure of the water in this river. It is a bit murky. I continue my thoughts trudging through the high grasses. Then, off to the side of me in the middle of this field, there is a herd of pronghorn! *¡Manada de berrendos!* How fortunate I am to have wandered out here at this time! They take no notice of me as I quietly make my way northward. It makes me happy to see the wildlife in this desert. I am surprised at the beauty which exists in this hot climate. I smirk when I think of the amount of rain I have endured in my travels. Flood and drought seem to be a way of life here.

CHAPTER 13

THE CREEK

The sound of voices knocks me from my reverie and I duck into the grasses. The sounds of chatter and laughter sound close but not too close, so I creep along low to the ground, hoping to see their location. As I peek out from behind a tree near the river, I can see a line of children in colorful clothing on the opposite side of the river. I duck back behind my tree and wait for them to proceed past. I can hear someone talking. I hear the words *Ciénega* Creek. I understand "one hundred springs" so I think he speaks of the river. I crouch and make my way back to the grasses and make haste to head north again. I do not know how many people come to this river but I am now nervous. To make things worse, I look up to see the clouds brewing overhead. On the bright side, a downpour will send most people running for shelter. With more rain my river will run more quickly, so I walk along the treeline with renewed focus. I am not in view of anyone walking along the river, so I can move more quickly. I am glad for the continued heat as I am now dry and feeling warm. The water will feel good once I can float again. When the trees start to thin out, my concern grows. I am not sure where to hide if anyone comes along. I follow the riverbed because it is my best hope for travel and water. With the gathering clouds I try to hurry to find the next group of trees. I may need to climb one!

I stop to sip more water. It is still very hot and I long for some shade now. I can see another treeline across the river from me, as though it lines yet another river, but I am unwilling to cross to the side where the people were hiking. I will keep following the river on this side. The wind picks up as I walk and this makes me walk faster. I have a sense of urgency and the weather is helping me with it. I can see trees in the distance and hope I will get to them soon. I also hope the river is moving more rapidly in that spot. The green of the trees gives me hope the water is more abundant there. My legs are tired but I keep walking. The clouds are now completely covering the sky above me, a very dark gray, almost black in places. A bright spike of lightning shatters the skyline. I start counting, *"uno, dos, tres, cuatro, cinco, seis, siete..."*. The thunder suddenly rolls deeply around me. The storm is just over a mile away. I want to run to the trees but I cannot. My body is weary and although the clouds did cool the temperature, I am still very hot. I keep my pace and soon enough I have reached the trees. Still the rains have not come. I am grateful the dust has not come.

The walk along the river bank is pleasant. I practice a new word. "Creek," I say out loud. Pleased with myself, I whistle a folk song my mother used to sing to me. The water here is flowing more rapidly than the segment I had floated a few hours previously. I think it will rain anyway, so I might get ahead of the storm by floating faster than I am walking. I need the rest anyway, so I make myself ready and jump in. This float starts off much more rapidly than the one before, so I find it harder to relax. Finally, as I get used to the rhythm of the stream, I feel my body go limp and my mind begins to enjoy the ride. I hardly notice when the rains begin. It feels like splashing from the river flow. Then as it begins to pound harder, it is harder to ignore. Thankfully I am able to catch my breath frequently as I pass under the canopy of the large cottonwood trees, because their branches slow the torrent. The waters are more choppy and I feel like I am on a wild ride. I think perhaps I should be afraid but I am not. I keep my toes pointed downstream and my hand on the raft. There doesn't seem to be a lot of debris in the water floating beside me, so it lessens my immediate danger. Truthfully I do not know what I will encounter downstream but my trip is going along very easily compared to walking.

I haven't seen any people since the group in the morning, so I think no one will be out in this storm. This sets my mind at ease. I realize as I relax that I am very hungry. I would very much like *champurrado*. Just to taste the thick hot chocolate and to feel it slide down my throat and warm my belly makes me moan. I will find this recipe one day, I promise myself. I continue my daydream until I realize it is no longer day. I must have floated for hours because I can now see stars in the sky. I do not know how deep the river is and I do not know if I should risk trying to stand and climb out. I cannot make out the banks. The river is not racing as quickly as it had been and I can't imagine I will get much sleep if I crawl out of the water and try to find a place to camp. The night air feels cool and so far the river feels warm. I will stay up this night and in the morning I will try to find a warm dry place to sleep and dry my clothing. This seems a sensible plan and I relax again for a long float.

My skin is like a dried prune. I crawl up the bank in the morning light. I do not know how far I roamed but I can hear traffic in the distance. Motors, not just a lone motor, drone continuously. I do not know what to make of this. I look across the river and see a hill. It would be best if I crossed to the other side so I can see what is going on. The last place I want to be right now is back in the water but I steel myself for it and walk across to the other side. It is very early morning and already it is getting warm so I am hopeful my clothes will dry soon. I climb the hill so I can view the terrain. With my compass I locate the area directly north which has the motor noise, so it must be a very large road! I do not want to enter the full desert without more water so I will have to trust the river water. I may have to cross that large road if I am to continue north, so for the time being I will go northwest and see what I find. I make my way back down to the water's edge. I fill one of my water bottles with the remaining rain water from the other. Then I fill the empty bottle from the river. Fortunately I have been drinking a lot of rainwater so I am not dehydrated for this trek. I set my compass and walk off into the hills.

CHAPTER 14

OVER THE RIDGES AND UNDER THE PASSES

It feels good to have the warm air on my skin. My clothes will be dry soon enough but in the meantime it feels like a nice breeze as I walk. There is not much to hide behind save an occasional bush or tree but there doesn't seem to be anyone out in this section of the desert. The motors in the distance are the only indication that people are nearby at all. I miss the seclusion of the trees by the river but I continue walking northwest, determined to make some good time. I am not sure why I need to go at any particular speed, but I guess the faster I get north, the further I will be from the bad men and from my native land. North is my symbol for freedom. It is my direction for a better life. I did not dislike the life I had with my parents, but my parents were determined that life would be even better - better if we went north. For them, I will pursue this dream.

The sun is approaching the 10 o'clock position and I am approaching a massive road! There are so many cars! I will not be able to cross this, I know it in my heart. I do see some large trees also near the road, so I walk toward those. At least I can hide there while I think about what to do. Perhaps there is a small pond or stream there. As I approach the trees, I can see a river next to them. It is flowing under the large road! I decide right away to float under this large road because there are many vehicles in this area and I am afraid there may be people around the road. I gather some leaves to place near my face. My frame is already filled with leaves and reeds so it looks natural, I imagine. I point my toes downstream and though the river is shallow, it does have a steady flow from the rains yesterday. It is now midday and there are not many trees overhead so I feel exposed as I float. As soon as I can get through this bridge area, I will try to walk in the trees again. I hope there will be trees to walk near. As I pass under the bridge, its shadow covers me. There are paintings on the cement as I float by. It is curious to see and I wonder how anyone managed to put them there. As I reach the other side, the darkening clouds have stretched across the sky above me. There has been a lot of rain on this trip! I notice the rains come in the afternoons. I have to choose whether to remain in the water or head for land. Since the river is somewhat shallow, the rains help its flow and perhaps it will carry me to a more protected area.

The silhouette ahead on the bank startles me. It is a man with a wide brim hat. It is not a Mexican sombrero though. He seems to be staring into the water. I do not know if I can get to the shore and escape his gaze. I pull the leaves closer to my head and dip my toes under the surface. I am nearing a bend and will be in his sight soon. A bright light illuminates the darkening sky and a loud "boom" follows it immediately. In that instant, the man jumps back from the bank, the rains pour down in a flood, and I am grateful for the leaves covering my face as I pass the spot where he stood a moment ago. I cannot be assured he did not see me, but I feel reasonably secure considering the deluge which is covering the area.

I can hear something ahead that has changed the tone of the river, so I carefully make my way to the bank. The river is moving more quickly and it is rising. I get out on the bank opposite of the side where the man stood. I do not know what I will encounter here but the sound the river is making gives me butterflies in my stomach. I stop to gather my belongings and thoughts. The straps of my frame are starting to wear so I loop new reeds. I gather some fresh reeds to weave with the ones attached to the frame. Some of the new reeds I can loop into the frame as well, making it feel more secure when I put it on my back. My supplies have dwindled but I still have plenty. The air is warm and the canopy of the trees above me keeps the downpour from being as severe. I can see the rain is heavy up the embankment. I will continue to follow the river and investigate the changes I hear. As I approach a more rocky area, the bank is growing steeper and the roar is louder. I can see a wall rise out of the river ahead, but barely. The river is about to spill over its top so the roar I hear is the river rushing up to hit this wall. I will have to climb and find somewhere to camp away from the river, since the rains are not abating and the river is still rising. I will need the remaining daylight to find a new place to set up camp. The climb out of this area is not easy. I wish I had been paying attention earlier when the walls were rising on either side of me. The rock I climb is slick. Climbing at an angle seems most prudent, so as I make my way up the walls I look down at the rising river, now cascading over the dam. I reflect on it: just as the wall is designed to keep water out of whatever lies below, so all the walls and barriers I encounter are doing the same for me. But like the water that just went over the top, I too will get past my barriers and make my way. Just as I am about to feel pleased about my thoughts, I reach the top.

More desert. I am happy to see the saguaro has bloomed though. Now it's fruit will be sweet and give me a nice drink. I wonder about the fruit still being there, with the rains and all, but I don't like to question providence. I must find a long stick to coax the fruit down. I head back toward the trees to look for a branch. The feeling comes upon me slowly. I can feel the eyes. I am being watched. My skin gets goosebumps, and my spine tingles. I turn very slowly. The dark beady eyes stare at me intently. I am looking directly into the eyes of my friend, the white rabbit. Granted, I assume it is my friend. Slowly I place my hands together like a prayer, and bow to my friend. *"Gracias, señor, por sus bendiciones constantes,"* I pray. My friend, like my God, has given me constant blessings and I am forever indebted.

Tucson, Arizona

CHAPTER 15

HOME IS WHERE YOU HANG YOUR PACK

The white rabbit begins to hop with hesitation. He stops to stare at me, before continuing his path westward. I watch him until I realize at his latest long pause, he expects me to follow. I gather my wits, forget about my search for a long stick, and run to catch up. He does not run from me but rather hops rapidly for a time and then sits to wait while watching me. We travel along like this as the sun begins to descend toward the horizon. He takes me along a gully for a while, then we again head west. As the sun is just going behind a distant hill, he enters a green yard. It is well tended and unfenced. Many of its neighbors have block fences or wood fences. This yard feels loved and open. I stand there staring at it, unaware someone is approaching me with a smile. "Hello," she says quietly, "Are you hungry?" She is holding out a *pan blanco*, a white bread is oblong, but this one is split and has a red meat inside. "My name is Elise," she says as I take the food from her.

I know I am not supposed to speak but it was irresistible, "Eelees," I try to say it like she does. She seems very happy I said her name. She is talking to me, I can tell, but I have no idea what she is saying. I try to eat and not make any eye contact. I am afraid, but more than that, I am tired and hungry. She is now beckoning me into the house. My eyes widen because I am unsure what I should do. It is almost dark and I have nowhere to camp. I decide to slip my frame off my back and place it against a chair. The house looks inviting. My own mother would never let me bring my frame into our simple home, and certainly not into such a place as this. Once inside, she gestures to take my pack but I cling to it, fearful of losing it. I cannot part with it. She nods and smiles and seems to understand.

She walks down a hallway pausing to make sure I am following her. I am not afraid, so it is a good sign. She opens the door to a room with a bed so large it almost fills it! It has cushions and blankets! She then shows me the bathroom and turns on the tap. A large shower of water suddenly appears so I know she wants me to bathe. Elise leaves the room and I close the door. I place my pack carefully in the corner behind the door, then take off all my clothing. I will wash them while I shower. There is a good soap bar already out, so I begin scrubbing as the water drizzles over me. As I lather my pants, I can see the stains are difficult but they are coming clean. I spend a long time getting each piece of my clothing clean and then concentrate on my body. My mother would work on my ears and behind them so I started with this task, trying to mimic what I remember her doing. Someone knocks on the door and I am so startled I almost fall but I catch myself and hop over the bathtub. There is a towel there so I wrap it around me and then peek out the door. Elise is there. She is speaking but I don't understand her. I just nod and she comes in and turns the water off, and without another word she leaves the room again. Once I am dry, I wrap the towel around my waist. I realize I cannot put the wet clothing on, especially with no breeze to dry me. I can't get into wonderful bed with wet clothing either.

My clothing is hung from a bar over the bathtub and I can see the water dripping onto the floor. This will not do! There is a smaller towel hanging so I put it on the floor to catch the drops of water. Then with a sigh, I leave the bathroom and walk toward the room with the giant bed. There on the bed is a t-shirt. There is also a pair of shorts seem large to me. I put them both on quickly and it feels good. Suddenly I stop short. I had forgotten my pack in the bathroom! I run out of the room to find Elise standing in the bathroom doorway, staring at my clothing. I can't even tell her I am sorry for the mess. I clear my throat so she will know I am here. She smiles at me. I walk past her, reach around the door and grab my pack. That was a close call. She is talking again and I try to understand. She walks to the kitchen and opens the refrigerator. She pulls out a bottle of milk. I have not seen milk in so long! My smile is wide as I watch her pour the milk into a glass. She pushes it toward me. Once I see it is mine, I take a long swallow, then another. In three drinks I have finished the milk, satisfied. She moves to pour some more into the glass but I hold up my hand to stop her. She smiles and puts the milk away.

She walks back down the hallway and pushes the door to

my room open again. Then she motions for me to follow her. She pushes open another door and there is a room filled with photographs, a large bed and other furniture. She is speaking to me and I am nodding. I hope I can one day understand the words. I turn to leave, trying to hide my embarrassment. I place my pack on the floor next to the bed and climb up. The bed is so soft. I feel my eyes closing just as my head touches the pillow.

The sunlight on my face awakens me and I stretch. I really don't want to leave this comfortable bed but I know I can't stay here. There will be questions about me I cannot answer. I bound out of bed with the thoughts and go to find my clothing. I hope they are dry now. When I push open the bathroom door, panic sets in. My clothing is gone! I walk out to the kitchen area. I can hear humming. Elise is there, down another hallway, folding my clothes! "Good morning!" she calls out when she sees me. I smile at her and wave. She hands me the stack of my clothes and motions for me to take them to my room. I set them on the bed and remove my borrowed clothes. My clothes feel soft and warm. They smell nice.

Elise is on the phone when I get to the kitchen. She smiles and makes a funny face while pointing at the phone. She pours a large glass of milk and slides it over to me. I sip this glass, savoring it. Her voice raises a little and I see her expression is serious. She is arguing with the other person, much I can tell. She has a finality to her tone as she slams the phone down. "I will not just hand you over to some other agency! I want to help!" Again, all I can do is nod. She suddenly smiles and says, "Come on! Let's go shopping!" She grabs my hand and we head for a door.

There in a large room is a car! Another large door opens and the sunlight makes the room bright. I shield my eyes. She opens the car door and motions for me to get in. We drive for a while, and Elise chatters. I stare out the car window as houses, and roads, and cars, and cacti and other objects go by. There are many huge bridges filled with cars, and the buildings seem to be getting larger. This must be a city. Our pueblo is small but my mother has told me about large cities. I could never have imagined this. I feel excitement as we stop in a large place filled with other cars, all in rows. My door opens and Elise takes my hand.

The shopping mall is overwhelming. I walk beside Elise and I feel very small. We go into store after store. She holds shirts up to me, making comments I can't understand. She points to colors. "Do you like the blue one?" I understood her! She points to a color and asks a question. That color is blue! I am so excited I nod and smile. I now have clothes of all different colors because I repeat this every time she asks. The pants she has me try on, so I have to go behind a curtain or a door to dress. She examines me and makes a grunt and puts them back on a hanger, or smiles and places them in a basket. She takes me to an area with many packs. All colors and sizes hang from rods. "Do you like any of these?" she is pulling them off one by one to show me. She unzips pockets, shows me the insides. There is one, it is larger than my current pack, but the same color. This one has more pockets. I really like it. I keep looking at it and inside it until she pulls it from my hands and it lands in the cart. "Let's go find shoes!" she announces and marches off toward another area, filled with *zapatos*. Shoes must be *zapatos*. "Do you like this shoe?" she is asking. My eyes wander, and I am amazed there are this many shoes in one place. My gaze settles on some black shoes with white stripes. "Nikes, huh? You have expensive taste! But good taste! That is an excellent choice." I am not sure what she said, but she has me sit down and a man comes over and places my foot on a metal bar. He moves some of the pieces until they touch my toes and the side of my foot. He then explains something to Elise, and leaves. He returns with a box. Out of the box he pulls those shoes! He puts one of them on my foot and pulls me out of the chair. He is saying something and demonstrating for me to walk. I walk a short way and he motions for me to sit again. He puts on the other shoe and tightens the laces on both. He pats the top of my foot, smiling. Elise carries the empty box to the register. I never saw my old shoes again.

Soon we are heading to the parking lot, with icy drinks in our hands. Elise is smiling and talking. I am smiling and nodding. She had me wear the last shirt and shorts we found. My clothes are in one of the plastic bags. I do not recognize myself. The ride home is another adventure, the sights astonishing. I am happy when I see a door opening and recognize the room where Elise puts her car. I feel exhausted, though I haven't roamed far or had to do any work. When I yawn, Elise takes my hand and walks me to my room. She points to the bed and says, "Nap time young man!" I crawl into bed, stretching. I don't think I have ever slept in the middle of the day. I don't dwell on the thought long. Soon, I am startled awake by the sound of voices. One of them is Elise. I wish I could understand. "Brad, I work for Social Services. I can take care of this child in the interim! Ryan and I will make sure he eats well, gets plenty of rest, visits a doctor, and a dentist, and we will try to get him enrolled in our elementary school! Until it is all sorted out, there is no reason to move him around more. If extended family members are found, we can worry about then!" I can hear her voice is very excited, but it is not happy sounding. A man's voice sounds closer. I quickly shut my eyes. I hear the door to my room open. I try to breathe deeply. I pretend it is my mother and I am tricking her into carrying me. "He does appear to be the age of the missing youngster," the man whispers, "No one figured he would be alive." I know something serious is going on but I also sense Elise is protecting me, so I don't feel fear.

The door closes and I let out a silent sigh of relief. I will wait for a while before I get up. I close my eyes and picture my mother. I am walking with her to do her rounds. She checks on the villagers, making sure they have medicine for their ailments. She examines them, laughs with them, and rummages through her bag to give them something to help them. I wonder what they will do now that she has left. I wonder what I will do now that I have left! I hear a soft knock and open my eyes. The bedroom door opens and Elise slips in. I look at her and smile. She smiles slowly and sits on my bed. Her finger curls my hair as she looks at me intently. "I have a lot of research to do. My husband comes home tonight. I will do my best to protect you," she speaks softly but with determination, much like my mother. I nod a little, and then close my eyes. I suddenly feel very tired, all over again. I don't want to run, even though I feel there is danger somehow.

When my eyes open again, Elise is talking rapidly but quietly in the other room. I walk out to the kitchen and see a man holding her. I guess he is her husband. After a short while she approaches me, speaking almost too loudly, "You are Gabriel! Aren't you? You just have to be! I know you are! You are Gabriel aren't you?" I don't really know what she is saying to me, and even though my mother gave me strict instructions never to speak, a smile involuntarily breaks out on my face. Gabriel is my best friend back home. He wanted to come with my family so badly but his family had nothing to trade for passage. I wonder if this woman knows my best friend. Could she have found him? It all seems incredible to me so I remain silent but grinning. She jumps and approaches the man. "Ryan, I think this is the little boy! The little boy they think burned in that fire in Naco! His family burned but he escaped! The report I read says the fire happened in the middle of the night and the whole family burned while sleeping! But, they never recovered the boy's body! They had to close the case eventually when no one had seen him and at his age it was largely believed unlikely he would have wandered off. boy was seven last year when the fire occurred. This boy seems to be about eight! It could really be him!"

She had a large manila folder under her arm and she opened it onto her kitchen table. I am staring at her, wondering what it all means. Her husband comes to stand over her and watches as she sorts papers. "This article announces the birth of Gabriel Martinez at the Copper Queen Community Hospital in Bisbee, Arizona. This one announces his baptism at St. Michael Catholic Parish in Naco! Ryan, Gabriel can get his life back now! If only I can convince them to let him remain with a social worker, we have a chance to give him a home. Get him enrolled in school!" "Elise, how much will this cost us?" the man is speaking quietly. "Will all your work make a difference?" Ryan looks at her pensively. I have no idea what they are saying but it seems like her husband is very serious, and as though Elise is very happy and excited. I remain confused but keep the smile on my face. I can still see Gabriel in my head, laughing in his great, hearty way. "Gabriel, are you from Naco?" Elise is looking directly into my eyes. "*Naco*," I repeat and nod. I think she is asking me if *Gabriel* is from *Naco*.

CHAPTER 16

BLOOM ELEMENTARY

Elise and I hold hands tightly as we walk into a classroom. The teacher appears nice. She is smiling at me. "Gabriel Martinez, you will sit here," The teacher points to a chair. I look around the room. My friend Gabriel is not here. And I don't know the name Martinez. I sit in the chair. The teacher and Elise talk for a moment and then Elise waves to me, "See you after school Gabriel! I will be here at 2:00!" In that moment, I realize they are calling me Gabriel. I will have to learn quickly. I have not been to school very often, usually I got my schooling from my mother. This school is American. They speak English. I will learn English! It is my mother's greatest dream for me.

I look into my old pack one day when I get home from school. I have not touched it since the day I arrived, months ago. I pull everything out. As I organize all of the herbs, I know I need a smaller medicine bag. I will ask Elise what I can use. Some things are shriveled up and I put those in the trash. In a smaller pocket I find the note my mother wrote. I open its worn and delicate paper. I can now read it! It says:

"I am an American." That is all it says. I think on this. This is what she wanted others to believe. This is what she wanted me to believe. "I am an American," I say out loud to no one in particular.

I walk to school every day. Next year, Elise says I can ride my bike to school. I have advanced to the third grade. I tested well, they said, so I need to be in a higher grade. Next year I want to test even higher! My life is easy. I have to keep my room clean. I have to rinse off my dishes. I have to shower each day and make my bed. I have to go to school and do my homework. The rest of the time is mine! I play baseball. I ride my bike. I am reading books in the "Chronicles of Narnia" series. I have a place in the corner of my room where I am hidden by my bed. I can turn on the lamp and read there, lying back on some large pillows.

I have made many friends and my entire focus is on learning English. I do not even speak in Spanish. I do not let on to anyone that I understand it and I sit and look blankly at anyone who begins to speak to me in it. My mother warned me and I believe my mother. I speak very little anyway, but when I do, I speak English. I have heard Elise talk about my trauma and she tells the school I am shy because of it. I am using this to my advantage to speak as little as possible until I understand more and can speak more clearly. I practice speaking English with younger children on the playground. Sometimes they even make fun of me and I avoid those mistakes in future conversations. My reading and writing is improving so rapidly that I am afraid I am drawing too much attention to myself.

I am making a private journal. In it I draw plants in colored pencil and neatly write their names in English and their names in Spanish. In English, I write what they cure and their benefits. Sometimes I know what to write about them but only in Spanish. This dilemma is soon solved when a friend introduces me to Google Translate. He is trying to help me learn Spanish. My new "parents" gave me a ProScan tablet with an attachable keyboard for Christmas this year, and I am constantly amazed at what is found on the internet. I do not get on the computer very often because I have so much to do outside my bedroom. I do enjoy translating the journal though, so Google Translate has its allotted time-slot, just before prayers and bed.

When I wake up one Saturday morning, there are voices in the kitchen. I jump out of bed, make it, grab a robe from the hook and put slippers on my feet. So long as I am covered up, I can investigate. Otherwise, I have to be fully dressed for company. I peek around a corner to see my school principal and my favorite teacher sipping coffee and laughing with Elise and Ryan. "Gabriel!" Elise cries out with a smile. She motions for me to come sit by her on one of the sofas. "Your teacher is just telling me about how talented a writer you are!" Elise beams down at me. Ryan laughs and gets up. "I'll get him an orange juice so he can wake up!" I think the word Americans use is "spoil" to refer to how I am treated. They really look after me.

"Gabriel, would you like it if Elise and Ryan adopted you?" the principal is asking. I want to tell her my parents are alive, but even this I do not know for sure. I want to tell her I am not Gabriel, but I know I cannot do this. I nod and smile. "Yes," is all I will say. She turns to Elise with a smile, "Then you have my blessing. I will write my letter of recommendation, as you suggest." At this time I am unaware the authorities have been unable to locate extended family for Gabriel Martinez, whose family had died in a tragic house fire in Naco, Arizona. Its sole survivor is presumed to be me, so without family and being so young, I will need to be given to a new family. My white rabbit led me to my new family.

In May during my fifth grade promotion ceremony from Bloom Elementary, I look out into the vast audience and see Elise and Ryan, both grinning from ear to ear. They don't look like my parents, but they sure act like them. When my name is called, "Gabriel Jordan," I can hear both of them hooting and hollering. I am proud to bear their name. I am now proud to be called Gabriel too. I am an American. And we are moving from Tucson, Arizona to Aspen, Colorado, where Elise has been promoted to a hospital administration position. We have hired movers, 'so we can concentrate on our good-byes and our special possessions' Elise informs me. I am only responsible for my treasures and my bags, which I have already carefully packed and stashed by the door. I see my bicycle carefully attached to the back of the moving van as it pulls out of our driveway. My excitement is building, as I can feel a new adventure looming. I can't wait to go to Colorado. And Colorado is even further north!

Aspen, Colorado

CHAPTER 17

ASPEN MIDDLE SCHOOL

I have gone from Elementary to Middle School, but the students here have been in Middle School since their 5th grade year. This does not bother me at all since I jumped into school from no school and passed through many of the grades. I enter my new school smiling. This is a magical place. Our house is on a side street off Cemetery Lane. There is a free bus to town, and the school bus picks me up a half block from where I live on school days. I had never ridden a bus until I came to this place. It is a new experience. My old school had alarms. Bells for everything. They chimed for ending classes, they chimed for beginning classes, they chimed for lunch and for dismissal. This school is amazing. There are no regular alarms. You are expected to go from one class to the next. Your teacher might say something different each day - each class - but it is the time on the clock which lets us know when we pack our bags, or when the teacher calls out that an upcoming assignment is due. I like this new method.

I have been assigned a buddy. His name is Rory. He has already been to my house. He says he is my reading buddy, but that we can hike and ski together too. I am most interested in the reading. I joined the book club at our school library. I hope one day I can read out loud without an accent. I will have to trust my buddy because it is a real opportunity for me to practice reading out loud for one hour a week. I have realized if I do this faithfully, my goal will be attained. Sometimes Rory tries to speak Spanish words to me. I stare at him. He stops. Thankfully, he doesn't ask.

Usually we go to the Pitkin County Library downtown to meet on Saturdays. If we meet during the week, we meet at the Middle School Library. I admit to Rory I don't believe my voice sounds right and I have trouble pronouncing words. He seems to think this is normal and we will have no trouble practicing our way out of it. His prognosis of the situation makes me happy. I feel like I will improve if he is willing to help me! When we get to the segment of our visit during which we read out loud, we usually go outside. If the weather is bad, we go over to a far corner inside the library and sit on bean bag chairs. I like it outside the best, since we can speak freely. I laugh when he teaches me the ABC song. I imagine small children learn this song. I do find it is helpful though, and find myself reviewing it in my head each day.

The librarian gives me books to read when I go to the Middle School Library. I read them at home and bring them back. Usually I bring them back the next day. One day, she tells me she really thinks I should go to the High School Library. She says she has already called ahead, and the librarian there will help me select some books. I go there directly after school. The librarian looks up and smiles. "Are you Gabriel?" I just nod and smile. There on her desk she pats a stack of books. "Please let me know what you think of these and also if any of them are too difficult." I take the stack of books and smile.

It's early Fall and a ski coach, Austin, approaches me about learning to ski. I have no idea what it is, but I have seen photographs and know you ski on snow. I have never seen snow. I do what I have learned to do successfully: I smile and nod my head in agreement. The coach looks very happy. He smiles back. "That's great!" he exclaims. "Once the snow comes we will practice on Saturdays! We start warm-ups in 2 weeks to get ready!"

Snow! I am standing by our window in complete awe. I can't move. The first snowstorm of the season hits in mid-October. The flakes are large and the ground is covered. I have never seen snow falling until now! I watch as the snowflakes hit the ground one after another, too many to count or see. Quickly, I don my jacket and race outside for a closer look. I catch some flakes in my hand and stare at them until they disappear. The whole world has changed. I barely recognize my neighborhood.

A teacher, Travis, stops me in the hall. He wants to know if I want to learn to ski. I told him about Saturday warm-ups and the other coach. He says he will give me additional lessons if I want. It will only be a few hours a couple of days a week after school. He gives me his phone number and I tell him I will call tonight after I have spoken with my parents. He pats my back. "Don't worry about gear!" he calls out as we part, "I can fit you on the first day and get a locker for you!" "Thanks!" I yell as I walk quickly down the hall to my next class. My mom is happy about the ski instruction. She is convinced I will love skiing and be good at it. I call the new "coach" to tell him the good news.

Ski practice is going very well. My after-school coach believes there is a lot of technique and even more natural talent involved in skiing. I am not afraid to try new things and I am not afraid to go fast. At first, he tried to get me to slow down. I think he is giving up. I have discovered moguls. Those are so fun! "Keep your brain bucket on, and focus on the run!" I always wear my helmet. I pay attention to my surroundings. Coach shakes his head as I careen toward him after blasting down a mogul filled run. He puts his arm over my shoulder as we stop for the afternoon. "You are a quick study. I think you can start practicing for the alpine races." Nothing pleases me more than knowing I can now join the others. He says he will consult with my AVSC coach and we will go from there.

On December 27th, the biggest snowfall of the season to date hits Aspen and our whole AVSC ski team is elated. We can't wait to hit the slopes. We had all trained and were ready for some of the expert slopes of Aspen Mountain. Coach is a little wary because of the number of us but it soon gives way to our excitement and his knowledge that we all have considerable skill. "This may be my best team ever," he mumbles as he starts to gather his gear. The storm is said to have dumped 25 inches of new powder, a new record. Since there was extensive snow fracturing seen near the top of Bell Mountain, we head over to Spar Gulch to make our runs there.

It is a total winter wonderland. Two more coaches have joined us so we split off into smaller groups. My after-school coach, Travis, and I are in the last group to ski down. I hang back with him, because I know he will watch the others start before he leaves. We start the run together. It is really fun and we begin to intertwine our runs. Suddenly there is a thunderous crash and a deafening roar from behind us. We both look up and see a massive avalanche of snow heading for us. I focus on my run and head straight down the mountain trying to keep to a side that is not in its direct path, although it appears the entire slope is in its direct path. This will be the ski race of my life, for my life!

Out of the corner of my eye I can see coach ahead of me and I pray he will not slow or turn on my behalf. I have no chance if I worry about him. Perhaps if I can ski faster than he does, he will then see me and keep outpacing the avalanche. I set my focus on outrunning my coach down the slope. Snow is now crashing on both sides of me as I lift airborne off a ridge. As I land, I am slightly in front of the coach and he and I begin a straight run, as though in a competition. As I ski away from a cloud of snow, I can see another on my other side. Each time I see a ridge, I head for it to launch over it. I can no longer see Travis. I have to just focus on my run. I am in a racing crouch with what seems to be two walls of snow on either side of me. I wonder if this is like skiing a chute.

As I come out of a mist of snow, I see a crowd of people before me clapping. I realize it is a huge audience, so I take a bow as I ski toward them. This causes an even louder and more enthusiastic response. When another roar comes from the crowd, I turn to see my coach tumbling out of the snow cloud. I ski toward him, along with several others. The ski patrol medics are telling him to lie still. His eyes meet mine and he grins at me. "You won!" I am relieved to hear him joking but I am unsure of his condition, so I give him a thumbs up before I back away.

I continue to ski and race with the team all season. Fortunately for my coach, Travis, he didn't have a neck or back injury but he does have to recover from a broken femur. I visit him often with tales from our competitions. I stick to groomed trails and normal ski days now. I avoid weather when skiing and I am not participating in Spring skiing. I have been reading up on avalanches.

I have joined the Aspen Skier Lacrosse Team. Although I have never played Lacrosse, my track records had arrived ahead of me and the coach asked me to join. We practice most days after school. Apparently I am a good defender on the crease and I am great on the fast break. There are new words to learn, and more importantly, new moves to learn. I am fast and I am strong. My lax coach seems to like me a lot.

CHAPTER 18

ASPEN HIGH SCHOOL

Book Club is going well. I have found a refuge in the library. When school is overwhelming or I need a place to hide, I find myself heading to the library. I am well known here. Sometimes, if I need a pass, the librarian winks and makes one out. I don't abuse it, but there are times when I simply get lost in a book and she seems to understand. One day, I will own a library of my own. I will have my favorite books there. I ask the librarian if we can keep a file on her computer with a list of my favorite books with author. I tell her I will bring books back in two stacks, favorites and others. She says she is happy to do it for me! When I reread an old favorite, I add it to my favorites stack so I can eventually add the books I had read previously to this list.

I met the former Pitkin County Sheriff, Bob, today at school after an assembly. We had a long discussion about a book I had read about hunting and fishing in the Roaring Fork Valley. He is going to take me hunting and teach me about gun safety and how to shoot a rifle. He says he also likes to fish and this makes me happy. I can go fishing with someone! We make plans for a few upcoming Saturdays. He gives me his phone number and tells me to have my mom call. My first time will be this coming Saturday and I can barely contain my excitement. He explains we will practice rifle and shotgun while the weather outside is still nice. Once the weather turns in late Fall, he says we will use handguns and an indoor range.

I still practice with the ski team, but I tell coach I will be working out on my own for warm-ups and will start my ski practices once the snow falls. This will give me extra time for my new interests. Once skiing starts in full force, I tell Bob I will have to put off my time at the range until Summer. He says it is good to take a break, let it all sink in. Between my current more difficult studies, my skiing, and my Lacrosse schedule in Spring, the school year passes quickly. I even lettered in Lacrosse and in Skiing my freshman year! I was told it is hard to do!

Summer in the Rockies seems to come late but once it hits, it is hard to beat! Hot days in beautiful surroundings! Bob and I have chosen a schedule so I can plan to be up early for target practice. He says it will get me into the habit for Fall hunting. He has an extra shotgun and rifle he brings along for me. I like the days when we do this because after we finish, he takes me to the Main Street Bakery for brunch. I had never heard of brunch until I met Bob. When I reflect on all the kindnesses this one man has shown me, it overwhelms me. One day I will show Bob my sketch book of herbs. Even though it is a prized possession of mine, I have never shown it to anyone but he seems to be a real friend.

I am almost 16 years old (I believe I am really almost 18 years old, given the years that have passed since I left my parents). I will be a Sophomore this year at Aspen High School. Bob and I have become good friends and this summer has been a great one! At one of our last brunches of the summer, I finally decide to pull out my book. "I wrote and illustrated this book, Bob," I tell him cautiously. He gets a curious grin on his face. "Let me see," he holds out his hand and leaves it there patiently. I place the book in his hand with some hesitation, fear mounting in my brain. I start to stutter and he holds up his hand. "It will be okay," he says gently. I watch as his eyes light up and his eyebrows raise and lower. "Wow!" is all he says as he finishes his brief perusal of its contents. "Where did you learn all of this?" he asks with a smile. I can see he is not interrogating me, but casually asking. "I started it when I was 8 or 10," I reply, not wanted to lie, "Some of the plant pictures I had to look up on the internet."

Because of my interest in his work as a Sheriff of Pitkin County, Bob suggests I talk to other officers about their jobs. He thinks I might enjoy being a police officer or sheriff one day. I have been talking to many police officers and sheriffs since. An Aspen Police Officer, Charlie, is helping me fill out papers so I can do a "ride-along" in the police car and see what a typical day is like. I have read a book about the Boy Scouts and their motto "Be Prepared". One day on a ride along I was thinking about the police department. I ask Charlie what their motto is. He laughs and replies, "Our mission is 'Policing committed to community needs.'" I think on this for a while. I have found it to be true with Charlie, Adam, and many others on this police force.

John, the manager of the local grocery, offered me a job today. I just turned 17 on November 3rd (as Gabriel Jordan). He shook my hand and told me to apply. Filling out the application did not look as easy as I thought it might, so I enlist Ryan's help. We sit at the computer to fill out the online application. My social security number is the first part that stumps me. "I think Mom got you one of those," Ryan says with a smile, "Let me call her at the hospital." He comes back with a folder. "She says it's in here!" Since I have had very little experience, work or otherwise, those parts of the online application go quickly. Once the application is completed, Ryan suggests I give it a day and then go into the market to see John. "To follow up," Ryan provides the words I can use.

Working in the grocery, I feel so proud. I have a job! I can save money. I can help to pay for future schooling, for my college. I am happy as I stock shelves and think of the possibilities. "Excuse me, do you work here?" From behind me I hear a woman asking. I turn with a smile, "Yes, how can I help you?" "Do you have horseradish?" she asks. I have never heard this word. I have no idea what she is asking. My look of panic must be saying it all. A man passing by says, "Apparently they do not have horseradish in Mexico." His simple words belittle me. Suddenly I feel as though my intelligence has been questioned. As though my being here has been questioned. I am left speechless. I need to go find someone who can help the woman. I turn to her, "I will be right back." I quickly move to find a manager. The Store Manager finds the woman and speaks to her. He smiles, he speaks kindly. I will tell you my observation of this manager: he is a peacemaker. I believe from my observing him from afar, he must be a child of God.

After a Saturday night ride along, Charlie offers to take me out to dinner. "What do you want to eat?" he asks. "Anything with horseradish," comes my quick reply. He studies my face, determines I am serious, and says, "Jimmy's it is then. Saturdays they have prime rib on the bar menu!" I don't really know what it means but I am hungry so I smile at him and my stomach growls. We are seated and open the menus. I close mine immediately. He looks at me quizzically, "Thought you were hungry?" "I am! I am ordering the prime rib and I want horseradish!" He laughs and puts his menu down. "Good choice!" He orders for the two of us. I am having water. I guess he didn't know I was truly serious about horseradish.

It is my junior year of High School, and my days and evenings are so full the time is flying by. The school is really big on college preparation and I can scarcely imagine attending college. I am determined to do everything that is expected of me to accomplish being ready for it though. My coaches think some schools with ski teams will be offering me scholarships. In our Discovery class, Melissa is helping me to learn how to apply to colleges, and how to best prepare for the ACT, a standardized test for college entrance. College seems like a long way off. I am honestly not sure if I should go to college. No one in my family has ever done this! Kathy set an appointment for mom and me to meet with her to discuss my path to college. She tells me there are first generation scholarships for students who are the first in their families to attend a college. She has many ideas for scholarships for which I should apply. She is so excited about this and it makes me smile. She is happy for me and it makes me want to go to college.

The thought of college, of my future, burdens me. During one of our Saturday brunches, I suddenly realize I want Bob to know my secret. The thought thoroughly surprises me. For a moment I think I must be crazy to even think of telling anyone, but I am bursting. I have so many hopes and dreams for the future but I cannot imagine a future without discovering the truth about what happened in my past. I miss my real parents. I have true concerns for them. I have no idea where they are or if they are even alive. They do not know what happened to me. I ask Bob if he has anywhere to be. He shakes his head, "Right here with you is all I have planned for my whole afternoon." I tell him I would like to take a walk with him and tell him a long story.

He listens mostly in silence as we walk and I talk. I tell him the entire story, from my childhood in Mexico through my arrival in Aspen. Other than an occasional "Wow!" or "Really?" he lets me drone on. When I am finished, he looks at me intently. All he says is, "I really want to help you." Once we get to my bus stop, he turns to me and says, "I will keep this in confidence unless I need to share it to get help, okay?" I nod, knowing my life will be taking another turn.

Desert Outside of Naco, Arizona

CHAPTER 19

HUNTING TRIP

It is the summer prior to my senior year. Bob announces we are going to Arizona to hunt in the desert! Some of his friends ask what we will hunt and Bob winks at me and says, "It will be a surprise!" I really have no other way to travel that far away from my family without leaving them. With this announcement, I can now accomplish my long-time desire and still be home with them the following week. Bob has convinced an old friend of his to come along, a man who once was in law enforcement in Mexico. He had come to the United States as a diplomat back in the 1970's and met Bob in Aspen. The two had remained close. *Jorge* had eventually moved to Aspen for his retirement, so Bob and George were able to continue their friendship in person. We opt to take Charlie's truck since it has a back seat, making a trip with four of us much more comfortable.

My parents are speaking to Bob, wanting him to assuage their last minute concerns. He assures them I have been properly trained and that we will do nothing unsafe. He promises to have me in bed at a reasonable hour. He does explain hunting has you up at the crack of dawn, so late nights are not really an option for old men. This seems to appease them, and they smile and wave their goodbyes. They had approved of the trip the week before when Bob called them, but watching us pack up with the rifles and all seemed to rile them.

We are driving all day Thursday to reach Phoenix. We plan to stay at a hotel before heading south to the desert southeast of Tucson. Bob will drive the first six hours, and Charlie the remaining six or seven, depending on how the roads are and how many stops we make. Bob whispers to me that he is happy to not drive after dark, since his eyes don't see as well at night any more.

Friday morning, we get up at 4:00 am. We head south out of Phoenix toward Tucson. We plan to start our hunt near the Naco border with Mexico, so we map our travels at a restaurant in Casa Grande. I am amazed at how quickly we will be there by truck. My travels had taken so long! By late morning we are near the border of Mexico. Using my memories and backtracking on some of my compass readings, we are going to try and reconstruct the location where I last saw my parents. We think we have found the section of road where the truck with flashlights passed me in the night. We then go back toward Naco, but not too far given the distance a young boy might be able to travel on foot. We find an old road and turn south on it. It seems to be a dead-end. We all get out to look around.

Charlie gives a shout as he is pointing and bending down. He finds a piece of cloth sticking out of the ground. He marks the spot with a pin. He then heads to the truck where he pulls out a shovel. He hands it to Bob, and grabs another shovel. We each follow him with our shovels and he gives us each a section to dig. We have instructions to do so very carefully and if we find anything at all, we are to stop and pin the position. What we would like to accomplish is to find out if there are bodies in the ground here and if we discover just one body, we plan to call in local authorities to retrieve it and analyze the area. We do not want to mess up a crime scene.

We all gently remove dirt in a grid around the piece of cloth which is visible. When George uncovers a decomposed hand, we stop. As a group from out of state, we don't want to split up, we don't want to leave the site, but we need to contact authorities and provide our location. Charlie gets on his radio and makes an attempt to contact someone at the nearest police station or on patrol. His first contact is a Border Patrol agent who is nearby. The agent tells Charlie he will assemble a team of various agencies who will want to be involved. Bob grins at Charlie, each knowing that the battle for the lead investigation has begun.

Soon the area is crawling with police, sheriffs, border patrol agents and last to arrive, the FBI. Jurisdiction is discussed. If international borders were crossed, the Border

Patrol or FBI would take the lead. What if they are locals? Ultimately, the FBI convinces all the others that the Federal Government will provide the resources and manpower needed to fully mark the grid, if this indeed proves to be a mass grave site. The agent points out they can also enlist Mexico's *Federales* if they need to do some investigation across the border. Given the testimony they are relying on is from someone who crossed the border with the alleged perpetrators, everyone gives in pretty quickly.

The actual "testimony" has come from Bob, "as told to him by a minor child". The FBI approaches him to speak with me directly, but Bob casually says, "I didn't say *he* was the boy. He is the child of some friends of mine. He is a junior at Aspen High School, expected to be graduated next year with honors. And probably with more than a few scholarships for academics, skiing, and Lacrosse." The agent then deadpans, "Will you please introduce me then to our other witness to this crime scene?" Not missing a beat, Bob exclaims, "Sure!" He and the agent come closer. Again, I do what I do best, I grin at him. "Pleased to meet you Officer -," I begin before he cuts me off. "Agent," he explains. "Pleased to meet you Agent Donnelly," I hold out my hand. "My name is Gabriel Jordan. I am an American." The whole thing just spills out of my mouth before I can add any filters. "Sorry son, I was not trying to dispute that," the agent sputters, by way of apology. So it turns out, it was exactly what I needed to say. I left it at that and I did not offer anything more. Bob looks approvingly in my direction later in the afternoon. He is really good at this.

The afternoon reveals several grids marking graves. Bodies are being carefully excavated. Coroners have been called in. They will work all night long if necessary. I know this because trucks with bright lights mounted are surrounding the area and the lights are being tested. Indeed, they have uncovered a mass grave site. I believe they will date this some ten years prior. I am sad, but have not lost hope. Having Bob, Charlie and George here will make the access to information much easier, since they are officially part of the investigation, even though none of them has any jurisdiction.

We have to end our hunting trip. I know I have to go home and tell my new parents the truth. With Bob at my side, I know we can make good decisions about the subsequent fall-out but I am truly afraid. I have actually told no lies, but I also have been complicit in my own identity allowances. While a smile and a nod can go a long way for a young boy, I am now becoming a man and the time has come to make a stand. Telling Elise and Ryan the truth, in English, will be the hardest thing I have ever done, bar none. Bob agrees to be there. He also will not be in a comfortable position, but he says he is ready to defend his stance. I believe him. I also feel sorry for him. I put him in this position.

The investigation reveals several Mexican Nationals among the dead. Not only does this give credence to my story (as told by Bob) but also it is found that the dating of the site is about 10 years earlier, thus further corroborating my story. The DNA testing is slow to come in but they also did not discover any young children or babies among the dead. *Elena* could be alive!

CHAPTER 20

TRUTH BE TOLD

We arrive at the house on Tuesday in the late morning. We have called ahead so Elise is off work and Ryan is fortunate because his work hasn't begun yet. They know there is something grave going on but they have no idea what it is. We have them sit comfortably. Then I begin to tell my story, from the beginning. When I get to the part where we find my father's body in the grave (his clothes worn by the corpse), they weep openly. I am weeping as well. The waves of its enormity are still crashing over my heart. I am able though, to recount that my mother and my sister are still unaccounted for, and this gives rise to a smile from all of us.

Once the mass grave site is cataloged, identified, and entered into evidence, the search for "survivors" begins, based upon the evidence relayed in the testimony. I will step forward eventually, to give my testimony in court, but it will be done under immunity granted by the FBI, once they have made a complete investigation. I know they did not find the bodies of my mother nor of my baby sister, so I am intent on finding them and grateful for the authorities who want to help.

The *Federales* have told the FBI they have found the perpetrator, but that he has surrounded himself with guards and with a woman and child, and they believe she and the child are about the ages described by the witness (me). They are investigating with extreme caution, they tell us, because the community is so small.

To extract my mother, the investigators believe I should be the one to lure her out of the house they plan to surround. They do not want casualties, and in particular they do not want any casualties to be the victims. None of us are sure my mother is the woman who is there, nor are we sure if the young girl they have spotted is my sister. Once the team is reasonably sure we have set up the best situation for all of us to go in, they radio for me to walk up the street and knock on the door. They didn't want the risk of sending me directly to the house, but I insisted, believing it gives my mother the best opportunity to get out alive. Also, I am still young and look less threatening approaching the house.

I cannot see any of the agents nearby. I have to just trust they are there. I walk to the front door of the house where the-man-with-the-scar lives. It is unlocked, so I carefully open it. I can't even imagine knocking. I peer around the corner of an alcove I had flattened myself into. There before me is my mother, yes, my own mother - older, but with her face. She is chopping onions (*cebollas* my favorite!). *"Mamá"* I whisper intently, *"Soy Alejandro."* Slowly she looks up, a slight smile on her face. She presses her finger to her lips, to silence me, gathers a scarf to tie on her head, and grabs her grocery shopping bag. She motions for me to follow and she leaves the same door I had just entered moments before. I follow her quickly, careful to be quiet.

She moves quickly down the block and I am now directly behind her. Suddenly from behind us I hear a man call out, *"¡Elvira!* As he shouts I move quickly and shove my mother into an alleyway. Just as I do this, I hear a shot ring out and it hits a building near us. Suddenly there is chaos. I hear gun shots all around, men shouting, and people running. The *Federales* have come through! I see uniformed men running up the street toward man's house!

My mother has been waiting for the day of her redemption since the horrible night when her husband was murdered before her eyes, the same moment her nightmare, what she felt as her lifelong betrayal of him, had begun. As she collapses weeping into my arms, I can feel her emotion escaping through me. *"Mamá ¿Dónde está Elena?"* I realize we still need to protect Elena from those who might want to harm her. An FBI agent walks over just as I am asking, "We waited until we were sure you were leaving with your mother, and then we went into the school to retrieve Elena from her classroom. We didn't want anyone having too much advance notice about it. If you both will come with me, we can go to the safe house." My mother smiles at him and I quietly translate his message for her.

Again, she begins weeping but gathers her things and stands. She takes my arm and gracefully walks with me, following the agent.

Elena is nine years old. I am desperately trying to do the math in my head, as Alejandro. I last saw them when I was ten years old and she was a newborn. I am now nineteen. My real age as a junior in High School. I will be a senior at age twenty. This is not a normal American age to be a High School senior. This makes me smile, since I am always doing something different. As we approach the safe house, I steel myself for someone I will not recognize but whom I know will be about my age when I left on this adventure.

They open a door for us and we enter. We are led to a room and asked to sit. A different door opens, and a small girl peeks out from behind a uniformed man. When I see her, I instantly cry out "Elena!" She looks like me! Okay, yes, she has on a dress, but it is my face I see! I don't want to scare her, so I approach her cautiously. She runs for me and holds me tightly. I hold her tightly to me. My mother is there too, all of us laughing, crying, and hugging.

Bob tells me George is working on two expedited temporary Visas so my mother and sister can be protected near me prior to any ensuing trials, thus allowing me time for reunion with them while I finish high school. He also tells me that my new parents, Elise and Ryan, are here but they do not want to interrupt. "Interrupt? Never! Tell them to get in here!" I cry out with a smile. I begin to tell my mother that my American parents are here. "*¡Mis padres americanos han llegado aqui, Mamá!*" When Ryan and

Elise enter the room, my mother rises with tears of joy rolling down her face. She moves to grab Elise' hands and holds them. *"¡Gracias por cuidar a mi hijo único como si fuera lo suyo!"* I translate for them as they stand there smiling at her. I relay her message, "She says 'Thank you for protecting and caring for my only son like he is your own'." Elise and Ryan both nod enthusiastically, exclaiming they are happy to have Gabriel, and feel fortunate to be a part of all of this now. As I translate, I see the look of confusion spread across my mother's face.

Explaining who I am, how old I am, what my name is - all details which should be commonplace - are now evolving into decisions I will have to make. Even if I went back to my original name, Alejandro, it would still change into Alex here in America. Once the families are settled, we will have to discuss all of it and try to come to a consensus so that no one feels left out or hurt. With all of this racing through my mind, I simply tell my mother we will discuss it all later. That now is not the time for her to worry. She accepts my words and places her head on my shoulder. I am now taller than my mother! This realization makes me smile. I hold out the arm on my other side to Elise, who comes right over to be next to me. I am surrounded by my family. They are all my family. I am Chicano.

ABOUT THE AUTHOR

Sheila O'Malley has a Bachelor of Arts Degree in Economics from the University of Colorado at Boulder, where she also studied International Relations and Spanish. She has lived in many parts of the United States, including Arizona. She and her sons currently reside in Aspen, Colorado.

www.ingramcontent.com/pod-product-compliance
Lightning Source LLC
Chambersburg PA
CBHW072007170626
46813CB00005B/2046